A GRANT OF ARMS

(BOOK #8 IN THE SORCERER'S RING)

MORGAN RICE

Books by Morgan Rice

THE SORCERER'S RING
A QUEST OF HEROES (BOOK #1)
A MARCH OF KINGS (BOOK #2)
A FEAST OF DRAGONS (BOOK #3)
A CLASH OF HONOR (BOOK #4)
A VOW OF GLORY (BOOK #5)
A CHARGE OF VALOR (BOOK #6)
A RITE OF SWORDS (BOOK #7)
A GRANT OF ARMS (BOOK #8)
A SKY OF SPELLS (BOOK #9)
A SEA OF SHIELDS (BOOK #10)
A REIGN OF STEEL (BOOK #11)

THE SURVIVAL TRILOGY
ARENA ONE (Book #1)
ARENA TWO (Book #2)

the Vampire Journals
turned (book #1)
loved (book #2)
betrayed (book #3)
destined (book #4)
desired (book #5)
betrothed (book #6)
vowed (book #7)
found (book #8)
resurrected (book #9)
craved (book #10)

"Mine honor is my life, both grow in one.
Take honor from me, and my life is done."

--William Shakespeare
Richard II

CHAPTER ONE

Gwendolyn braced herself against the cold, whipping wind as she stood at the edge of the Canyon and took her first step onto the arched footbridge that spanned the Northern Crossing. This rickety bridge, covered in ice, was comprised of a worn wooden rope and planks, and hardly seemed capable of holding them. Gwen cringed as she took her first step.

Gwen slipped, and reached out and grabbed the railing, which swung and hardly helped. Her heart dropped to consider that this flimsy bridge was their only way to cross the northern side of the Canyon, to enter the Netherworld, and to find Argon. She looked up and saw, in the distance, the Netherworld beckoning, a sheet of blinding snow. The crossing felt even more ominous.

A sudden gale came, and the rope swayed so violently, Gwendolyn felt herself grabbing the rail with both hands and dropping to her knees. For a moment she did not know if she could even hang on—much less cross it. She realized this was far more dangerous than she had thought, and that they would all be taking their lives into their hands to try.

"My lady?" came the voice.

Gwen turned to see Aberthol standing a few feet away, beside Steffen, Alistair and Krohn, all of them waiting to follow. The five of them made an unlikely group, perched here on the edge of the world, facing an uncertain future and a probable death.

"Must we really attempt to cross this?" he asked.

Gwendolyn turned and looked back out at the whipping snow and wind before her, and clutched her furs tighter around her shoulders as she shivered. Secretly, she did not want to cross it; she did not want to take this journey at all. She would so much rather retreat to the safety of her childhood home, King's Court, to sit behind its snug walls, before a fire, and contemplate none of the dangers and worries of the world that had engulfed her since she had become queen.

But of course, she could not do that. King's Court was no more; her childhood was gone; and she was Queen now. She had a baby-to-be to care for, a husband-to-be out there somewhere, and they needed her. For Thorgrin, she would walk through fire if that was needed.

Gwen felt certain that it was indeed needed. They all needed Argon—not just her and Thor, but the entire Ring. They were up against not only Andronicus, but also a powerful magic, powerful enough to ensnare Thor, and without Argon, she did not know how they could possibly combat it.

"Yes," she replied. "We must."

Gwen prepared to take another step, and this time Steffen rushed forward, blocking her way.

"My lady, please allow me to go first," he said. "We do not know what terrors await us on this bridge."

Gwendolyn was touched by his offer, but reached up and gently pushed him aside.

"No," she said. "I shall."

She waited no longer, but stepped forward, grabbing firm hold of the rope rail.

As she took a step, she was struck by the freezing sensation in her hand, the ice digging into her, the cold sensation shooting up her palms and arms. She breathed sharply, unsure if she could even hang on.

Another gale of wind came, blowing the bridge side to side, forcing her to grab harder, to tolerate the pain of the ice. She struggled to balance with all she had, as her feet slipped on the ice-covered rope and planks beneath her. The bridge lurched sharply to the left, and for a moment she was sure she would fall over the side. The bridge corrected itself, and swayed back in the other direction.

Gwen knelt again. She had barely gone ten feet, and already her heart was pounding so hard she could barely breathe, and her hands were so numb she could hardly feel them.

She closed her eyes and took a deep breath, and she thought of Thor. She pictured his face, every angle of it. She dwelled on her love for him. Her determination to free him. Whatever it took.

Whatever it took.

Gwendolyn opened her eyes and forced herself to take several steps forward, clutching the railing, not willing to stop this time for anything. The wind and snow could drive her down into the depths of the Canyon. She no longer cared. It was no longer about her; it was about the love of her life. For him, she could do anything.

Gwendolyn felt the weight shift on the bridge behind her, and she glanced back to see Steffen, Aberthol, Alistair and Krohn following. Krohn slipped on his paws as he rushed past the others, weaving in and out until he was by Gwendolyn's side.

"I don't know if I can do this," Aberthol called out, his voice strained, after a few shaky steps.

He stood there, arms shaking as he clutched the rope, a feeble old man, barely able to hang on.

"You can do it," Alistair said, stepping up beside him and draping one arm around his waist. "I'm right here. Do not worry."

Alistair walked with him, helping him forward as the group resumed walking, heading farther and farther across the bridge, one step at a time.

Gwen once again marveled at Alistair's strength in the face of adversity, her calm nature, her fearlessness. She also exuded a power that Gwendolyn did not understand. Gwen could not explain why she felt as close to her as she did, but in the short time she had known her, she already felt like a sister. She drew strength from her presence. And from Steffen's.

There came a lull in the wind, and they made good time. Soon they crossed the midpoint of the bridge, moving faster now, Gwen getting a hang of the slippery planks. The far side of the Canyon began to come into sight, only fifty yards away. Gwendolyn's heart began to well with optimism. They might make it after all.

A fresh gale whipped through, this one stronger than all the others, so strong that Gwen was forced to drop to her knees and clutch the rope with both hands. She held on for dear life as the bridge swung up nearly ninety degrees, then swung back down just as violently. She felt a plank give way beneath her feet, and she cried out as one of her legs sank down into the opening, through the bridge, her leg stuck up to her thigh. She wiggled, but could not get out.

Gwendolyn turned to watch Aberthol lose his grip, letting go of Alistair and beginning to slide over the edge of the bridge. Alistair reacted quickly, reaching out with one hand and clasping his wrist, holding him back just before Aberthol slipped over the edge.

Alistair leaned over the edge of the bridge, holding on, as Aberthol swung beneath her, nothing between him and the bottom of the Canyon. Alistair strained, and Gwen prayed the rope did not give. Gwen felt so helpless, stuck as she was, her leg lodged between the planks. Her heart pounded madly as she tried to get out.

The bridge swayed wildly, and Alistair and Aberthol swayed with it.

"Let go!" Aberthol screamed. "Save yourself!"

Aberthol's cane slipped from his hand and tumbled through the sky, end over end, down towards the depths of the Canyon. Now all he had left was the staff strapped to his back.

"You are going to be okay," Alistair said calmly.

Gwen looked over, surprised to see Alistair so poised, confident.

"Look into my eyes," Alistair instructed, firmly.

"What?" Aberthol screamed out over the wind.

"Look into my eyes," Alistair commanded, even more strength in her voice.

There was something about her tone that commanded men, and Aberthol looked up at her. Their eyes locked, and as they did, Gwendolyn watched a light glow emanate from Alistair's eyes and shine down to Aberthol's. She watched in disbelief as the glow enveloped Aberthol, and as Alistair leaned back and with one yank, pulled Aberthol back up, onto the bridge.

Aberthol, stunned, lay there, breathing hard, and looked up at Alistair in wonder; then he immediately turned and grabbed hold of the rope railing with both hands, before another gust of wind came.

"My lady!" Steffen yelled.

Gwen looked over to see him kneeling over her. He reached down, grabbed her shoulders, and yanked with all his might.

Gwen began to slowly dislodge from the planks, but as she came close to breaking free, she slipped from his icy grip and slipped back down to where she was, lodged even deeper. Suddenly, a second plank beneath Gwendolyn snapped, and she screamed as she felt herself begin to plummet.

Gwendolyn reached up and grabbed hold of the rope with one hand, and Steffen's wrist with the other. She felt as if her shoulders were being torn from her sockets as she dangled in the open air. Steffen dangled now, too, leaning so far over the edge, his legs tangled up behind him, risking his life to keep her from falling, the breaking ropes behind him the only thing keeping them afloat.

There came a snarling and Krohn leapt forward and sunk his fangs into the fur on Gwen's coat and pulled back with all he had, snarling and whining.

Slowly, Gwen was hoisted, inch by inch, until finally she could grab hold of the planks on the bridge. She dragged herself up and lay there face first, spent, breathing hard.

Krohn licked her face again and again, and she breathed, so grateful for him, and for Steffen, who now lay beside her. She was so happy to be alive, to be saved from a horrible death.

But Gwendolyn suddenly heard a snapping noise, and felt the entire bridge quiver. Her blood ran cold as she turned and looked back: one of the ropes anchoring the bridge to the Canyon snapped off.

The entire bridge jerked, and Gwen watched in horror as the other one, hanging by a thread, snapped, too.

They all screamed as suddenly half of the entire bridge detached from the Canyon wall; the bridge swung them all so fast that Gwen could hardly breathe as they flew through the air, heading at light speed for the far side of the Canyon wall.

Gwen looked up and saw the rock wall coming at them in a blur, and she knew that in moments, they would all be dead from the impact, their bodies crushed, and that whatever survived of them would plummet down to the depths of the earth.

"Rock, give way, I COMMAND YOU!" shouted a voice filled with ancient primordial authority, a voice unlike any Gwen had ever heard.

She glanced over to see Alistair, clutching the rope, holding out one palm, fixated fearlessly on the cliff they were about to hit. From Alistair's palm there emanated a yellow light, and as they sped closer to the Canyon wall, as Gwendolyn braced herself for impact, she was shocked at what happened next.

Before her eyes, the solid rock face of the Canyon changed to snow—as they all impacted, Gwendolyn did not feel the crack of bones she had expected to. Instead, she felt her entire body immersed in a wall of light fluffy snow. It was freezing, and it covered her completely, entering her eyes and nose and ears—but it did not hurt her.

She was alive.

They all dangled there, the rope hanging from the top of the Canyon, immersed in the wall of snow, and Gwendolyn felt a strong hand grab her wrist. Alistair. Her hand was strangely warm, despite the freezing cold. Alistair had already somehow grabbed the others, too, and soon they were all, including Krohn, yanked up by her, as she climbed the rope as if it were nothing.

Finally, they reached the top, and Gwen collapsed on solid ground, on the far side of the Canyon. The second they did, the rope snapped, and what was left of the bridge plummeted down, hurling into the mist, into the depths of the Canyon.

Gwendolyn lay there, breathing hard, so grateful to be on solid ground again, wondering what just happened. The ground was freezing, covered in ice and snow, but nonetheless it was solid ground. She was off the bridge, and she was alive. They had made it. Thanks to Alistair.

Gwendolyn turned and looked over at Alistair with a new sense of wonder and respect. She was beyond grateful to have her by her side. She felt like the sister she'd never had, and Gwen had a feeling that she had not even begun to see the depth of Alistair's power.

Gwen had no idea how they would make it back to the mainland of the Ring when they were done here—*if* they were ever done, if they ever even found Argon and made it back. And as she peered into the wall of blinding snow ahead of her, the entry to the Netherworld, she had a sinking feeling that the hardest obstacles still lay before them.

CHAPTER TWO

Reece stood on the Eastern Crossing of the Canyon, clutching onto the stone railing of the bridge, and looking down over the precipice in horror. He could hardly breathe. He still could not believe what he had just witnessed: he had watched the Destiny Sword, lodged in the boulder, plummet over the edge, tumble end over end, dropping like a cannonball, swallowed by the mist.

He had waited and waited, expecting to hear the crash, to feel the tremor beneath his feet. But to his shock, the noise never came. Was the Canyon indeed bottomless? Were the rumors true?

Finally, Reece let go of the railing, his knuckles white, released his breath, and turned and looked at his fellow Legion. They all stood there—O'Connor, Elden, Conven, Indra, Serna and Krog—also looking over, aghast. The seven of them stood frozen in place, none able to comprehend what had just happened. The Destiny Sword; the legend they had all grown up with; the most important weapon in the world; the property of kings. And the only thing left keeping the Shield up.

It had just slipped from their grasp, descended into oblivion.

Reece felt he had failed. He felt he had let down not just Thor, but the entire Ring. Why couldn't they have gotten there just a few minutes sooner? Just a few more feet, and he would have saved it.

Reece turned and looked at the far side of the Canyon, the Empire side, and he braced himself. With the Sword gone, he expected the Shield to lower, expected all the Empire soldiers lined up on the other side to suddenly stampede and cross into the Ring. But a curious thing happened: as he watched, none of them entered the bridge. One of them tried, and was eviscerated.

Somehow, the Shield was still up. He did not understand.

"It makes no sense," Reece said to the others. "The Sword has left the Ring. How can the Shield still be up?"

"The Sword has not left the Ring," O'Connor suggested. "It has not crossed yet to the other side of the Ring. It has fallen straight down. It is stuck between two worlds."

"Then what becomes of the Shield if the Sword is neither here nor there?" Elden asked.

They all looked at each other in wonder. No one held the answer; this was all unexplored territory.

"We can't just walk away," Reece said. "The Ring is safe with the Sword on our side—but we don't know what will happen if the Sword lingers below."

"As long as it is not in our grasp, we don't know if it can end up on the other side," Elden added, agreeing.

"It is not a chance we can take," Reece said. "The fate of the Ring rests on it. We cannot return empty-handed, as failures."

Reece turned and looked at the others, decided.

"We must retrieve it," he concluded. "Before someone else does."

"*Retrieve* it?" Krog asked, aghast. "Are you a fool? How exactly do you plan to do that?"

Reece turned and stared down Krog, who stared back, defiant as always. Krog had become a real Thorn in Reece's side, defying his command at every turn, challenging him for power at every corner. Reece was losing patience with him.

"We will do it," Reece insisted, "by descending to the bottom of the Canyon."

The others gasped, and Krog raised his hands to his hips, grimacing.

"You are mad," he said. "No one has ever descended to the bottom of the Canyon."

"Nobody knows if there even *is* a bottom," Serna chimed in. "For all we know the Sword descended into a cloud, and is still descending as we speak."

"Nonsense," Reece countered. "Everything must have a bottom. Even the sea."

"Well, even if the bottom does exist," Krog retorted, "what good does it do us if it so far down that we can neither see nor hear it? It could take us days to reach it—*weeks*."

"Not to mention, it's hardly a leisurely hike," Serna said. "Have you not seen the cliffs?"

Reece turned and surveyed the cliffs, the ancient rock walls of the canyon, partially concealed in the swirling mists. They were straight, vertical. He knew they were right; it would not be easy. Yet he also knew that they had no choice.

"It gets worse," Reece retorted. "Those walls are also slick with mist. And even if we do reach the bottom, we might not ever get back up."

They all stared at him, puzzled.

"Then you yourself agree that it is madness to try," Krog said.

"I agree it is madness," Reece said, his voice booming with authority and confidence. "But madness is what we were born for. We are not mere men; we are not mere citizens of the Ring. We are a special breed: we are soldiers. We are warriors. We are men of the Legion. We took a vow, an oath. We vowed to never shy from a quest because it is too difficult or dangerous, to never hesitate because an endeavor may cause personal harm. It is for the weak to hide and cower—not for us. That is what *makes* us warriors. That is the very essence of valor: you embark on a cause bigger than yourself because it is the right thing to do, the honorable thing to do, even if it may be impossible. After all, it is not the achieving that makes something valorous, but the attempting of it. It is bigger than us. It is *who we are*."

There came a heavy silence, as the wind whipped through and the others contemplated his words.

Finally, Indra stepped forward.

"I am with Reece," she said.

"As am I," Elden added, stepping forward.

"And I," O'Connor added, stepping to Reece's side.

Conven walked silently beside Reece, gripping the hilt of his sword, and turned and faced the others. "For Thorgrin," he said, "I would go to the ends of the earth."

Reece felt emboldened having his tried-and-true Legion members at his side, these people who had become as close to him as family, who had ventured with him to the ends of the Empire. The five of them stood there and stared back at the two new Legion members, Krog and Serna, and Reece wondered if they were going to join them. They could use the extra hands; but if they wanted to turn back, then so be it. He would not ask twice.

Krog and Serna stood there, staring back, unsure.

"I am a woman," Indra said to them, "as you have mocked me before. And yet here I stand, ready for a warrior's challenge—while there you are, with all your muscles, mocking and afraid."

Serna grunted, annoyed, brushing back his long brown hair from his wide, narrow eyes and stepping forward.

"I will go," he said, "but only for Thorgrin's sake."

Krog was the only one who stood there, red-faced, defiant.

"You are damn fools," he said. "All of you."

But still, he stepped forward, joining them.

Reece, satisfied, turned and led them to the Canyon's edge. There was no more time to waste.

*

Reece clung to the side of the cliff as he inched his way down, the others several feet above him, all of them climbing their way painfully down, as they had been for hours. Reece's heart pounded as he scrambled to keep his footing, his fingers raw and numb with cold, his feet slipping on the slick rock. He had not anticipated it to be this hard. He had looked down and had studied the terrain, the shape of the rock, and had noticed that in some places, the rock went straight down, perfectly smooth, impossible to climb; in other places it was covered in a dense moss; and in still others, it had a serrated slope, indents, holes, nooks and crannies in which one could place one's feet and hands. He had even spotted the occasional ledge to rest on.

Yet the actual climbing had proved much harder than it had seemed. The mist perpetually obscured his view, and as Reece swallowed and looked down, he was having a harder and harder time finding footholds. Not to mention, even after all this time climbing, the bottom, if it even existed, remained out of sight.

Inwardly, Reece was feeling a mounting fear, a dryness in his throat. A part of him wondered if he had made a grave mistake.

But he dared not show his fear to the others. He was their de factor leader now, and he needed to set an example. He also knew that indulging his fears would not do him any good. He needed to stay strong and to stay focused, and he knew that fear would only obscure his abilities.

Reece's hands were trembling as he got a hold of himself. He told himself he had to forget what lay below and concentrate just on what lay before him.

Just one step at a time, he told himself. He felt better thinking of it that way.

Reece found another foothold, and took another step down, then another, and found himself starting to get back into a rhythm.

"WATCH OUT!" someone yelled.

Reece braced himself as small pebbles suddenly showered down all around him, bouncing off his head and shoulders. He looked up to see a large rock come hurling down, and he dodged and just missed it.

"Sorry!" O'Connor called down. "Loose rock!"

Reece's heart was pounding as he looked back down and tried to stay calm. He was dying to know where the bottom was; he reached over, grabbed a small rock which had landed on his shoulder, and, looking down, hurled it.

He watched, waiting to see if it made a noise.

It never did.

His foreboding deepened. There was still no sense of where the bottom was. And with his hands and feet already trembling, he did not know if they could make it. Reece swallowed, all sorts of thoughts racing through his brain as he continued. What if Krog had been right? What if there really was no bottom? What if this was a reckless suicide mission?

As Reece took another step, scampering down several feet, gaining momentum again, suddenly he heard the sound of body scraping rock, and then heard someone cry out. There came a commotion beside him, and he looked over to see Elden, beginning to fall, slipping down past him.

Reece instinctively reached out a hand, and managed to grab Elden's wrist as he slipped past. Luckily Reece had a firm grip on the cliff with his other hand, and he was able to hold with Elden tightly, preventing him from sliding all the way down. Elden dangled, though, unable to find footing. Elden was too big and heavy, and Reece felt his strength slipping away.

Indra appeared, scaling down quickly, and she reached out and grab Elden's other wrist. Elden scrambled, but could not find footing.

"I can't find a hole!" Elden screamed back, panic in his voice. He kicked wildly, and Reece feared that he would lose his own grip and go falling down with him. He thought quickly.

Reece recalled the rope and grappling hook that O'Connor had shown him before their descent, the tool of choice they used to scale walls during a siege. *In case it comes in handy*, O'Connor had said.

"O'Connor, your rope!" Reece screamed. "Throw it down!"

Reece looked up and watched O'Connor pull the rope from his waist, lean back and impale the hook into a nook in the wall. He sank it in with all his might, tested it several times, then threw it down. The rope dangled past Reece.

It couldn't have come a moment sooner. Elden's slippery palm was sliding out of Reece's hand, and as he began to fall back, Elden reached out and grabbed the rope. Reece held his breath, praying it held.

It did. Elden slowly pulled himself up, until finally he found a strong footing. He stood on a ledge, breathing hard, back to his old balance. He breathed a deep sigh of relief, and so did Reece. It had been too close a call.

*

They climbed and climbed, until Reece did not know how much time had passed. The sky turned darker, and Reece dripped with sweat despite the cold, feeling as if any moment could be his last. His hands and feet shook violently, and the sound of his own breathing filled his ears. He wondered how much more of this he could take. He knew that if they do not find the bottom soon, they would all have to stop and rest, especially as it would be dark soon. But the problem was, there was nowhere to stop and rest.

Reece could not help but wonder, if they all became too exhausted, if the others might just begin to fall, one at a time.

There came a great clamor of rock, and a small avalanche came, tons of pebbles raining down, landing on Reece's head and face and eyes. His heart stopped as he heard a scream—a different one this time, a scream of death. Out of the corner of his eye he saw plummeting past him, almost faster than he could process, a body.

Reece reached out a hand to grab him, but it happened too fast. All he could do was turn and watch as he spotted Krog, airborne, flailing, shrieking, falling back first, straight down into nothingness.

CHAPTER THREE

Kendrick sat astride his horse, beside Erec, Bronson, Srog, out in front of his thousands of men as he faced down Tirus and the Empire. They had walked right into a trap. They had been sold out by Tirus, and Kendrick realized now, too late, that it had been a great mistake to trust him.

Kendrick looked up and to his right, and saw ten thousand Empire soldiers up high on the ridge of the valley, arrows at the ready, and he looked to his left and saw just as many. Before them stood even more. Kendrick's few thousand men could never possibly outfight this number of soldiers. They would be slaughtered to even try. And with all those bows drawn, the slightest move would result in the massacre of his men. Geographically, being at the base of a valley, didn't help them either. Tirus had chosen his ambush location well.

As Kendrick sat there, helpless, his face burning with rage and indignation, he stared back at Tirus, who sat up high on his horse with a self-satisfied smile. Beside him sat his four sons, and beside them, an Empire commander.

"Is money that important to you?" Kendrick asked Tirus, hardly ten feet away, his voice as cold as steel. "Would you sell your own people, your own blood?"

Tirus showed no remorse; he smiled still wider.

"Your people are not my blood, remember?" he said. "That is why I am not, according to your laws, entitled to my brother's throne."

Erec cleared his throat in anger.

"The MacGil laws pass the throne to the son—not to the brother."

Tirus shook his head.

"All inconsequential now. Your laws no longer matter. Might always triumphs over law. It is those with might who dictate the law. And now as you can see, I am stronger. Which means, from now on, I write the law. Succeeding generations will remember none of your laws. All that they will remember is that I, Tirus, was King. Not you, and not your sister."

"Thrones taken by illegitimacy never last," Kendrick countered. "You may kill us; you may even convince Andronicus to grant you a throne. But you and I both know you won't rule for long. You'll be betrayed by the same treachery you instilled on us."

Tirus sat there, unfazed.

"Then I shall savor those brief days on my throne while they last—and I shall applaud the man that can betray me with as much skill in which I have betrayed you."

"Enough talk!" the Empire commanders yelled out. "Surrender now or your men will die!"

Kendrick stared back, furious, knowing he needed to surrender but not wanting to.

"Lay down your arms," Tirus said calmly, his voice reassuring, "and I will treat you fairly, as one warrior to another. You shall be my prisoners of war. I may not share your laws, but I do honor the battle code of a warrior. I promise you, you shall not be harmed under my watch."

Kendrick looked over at Bronson, at Srog and at Erec, who glanced back at him. All of them sat there, proud warriors each, horses prancing beneath them, silent.

"Why should we trust you?" Bronson called out to Tirus. "You who have already proven that your word means nothing. I am of a mind to die here on the battlefield, just to wipe that smug smile off your face."

Tirus turned and scowled at Bronson.

"You speak though you are not even a MacGil. You are a McCloud. You have no right interfering in MacGil business."

Kendrick came to the defense of his friend: "Bronson is as much a MacGil now as any of us. He speaks with the voice of our men."

Tirus gritted his teeth, clearly annoyed.

"The choice is yours. Look all about you and see our thousands of archers at the ready. You have been outwitted. If you even reach for your swords, your men will fall dead on the spot. Surely even you can see that. There are times to fight, and times to surrender. If you want to protect your men, you will do what any good commander would do. Lay down your arms."

Kendrick clenched his jaw several times, burning up inside. As much as he hated to admit it, he knew Tirus was correct. He glanced about and knew in an instant that most if not all of his men would die here if they tried to fight. As much as he wanted to fight, he knew that it would be the selfish choice; and as much as he despised Tirus, he sensed that he was telling the truth and that his men would not be harmed. As long as they lived, they could always fight another day, in some other place, on some other battlefield.

Kendrick looked over at Erec, a man he had fought with countless times, the champion of the Silver, and he knew that he was thinking the same thing. It was different to be a leader than to be a warrior: a warrior could fight with reckless abandon, but a leader had to think of others first.

"There is a time for arms, and a time for surrender," Erec called out. "We will take you for your word as a warrior that our men shall be unharmed, and on that condition, we will lay down our arms. But if you violate your word, God rest your soul, I will come back from hell to avenge each and every one of my men."

Tirus nodded, satisfied, and Erec reached out and dropped his sword and scabbard, down to the ground. It landed with a clang.

Kendrick followed, as did Bronson and Srog, each of them reluctant but knowing it was the wise course. All of their swords landed with a clang.

Behind them came the clang of thousands of weapons, all falling through the air and landing on the winter ground, all of the Silver and MacGils and Silesians surrendering.

Tirus smiled wide.

"Now dismount," he commanded.

One at a time, they dismounted, standing before their horses.

Tirus grinned, reveling in his victory.

"For all those years I was exiled to the Upper Isles, I envied King's Court, my elder brother, all of his power. But now which MacGil holds all the power?"

"The power of treachery is no power at all," Bronson said back.

Tirus scowled and nodded to his men.

They rushed forward and bound each of their wrists with coarse ropes. They all began to get dragged away, thousands of them, captives.

As Kendrick was being pulled, he suddenly recalled his brother, Godfrey. They had all set off together, yet he had not seen him or his men anywhere since. He wondered if somehow he had managed to escape? He prayed that he would find a better fate than they. Somehow, he was optimistic.

With Godfrey, one never knew.

CHAPTER FOUR

Godfrey rode out in front of his men, flanked by Akorth, Fulton and his Silesian general, and riding beside the Empire commander whom he had paid off liberally. Godfrey rode with a wide smile on his face, more than satisfied as he looked over and saw the division of Empire men, several thousand strong, riding alongside them, joining his cause.

He reflected with satisfaction on the payoff he had given them, the endless bags of gold, recalled the look on their faces, and was elated that his plan had worked. He hadn't been sure of it up until the last moment, and for the first time, he breathed easy. There were many ways to win a battle, after all, and he had just won one without shedding a drop of blood. Perhaps that didn't make him as chivalrous or bold as the other warriors. But, still, it made him successful. And at the end of the day, wasn't that the goal? He would rather keep all his men alive with a little bit of bribery than see half of them killed in some reckless act of chivalry. That was just him.

Godfrey had worked hard to achieve what he had. He'd used all of his black-market connections, through the brothels, back alleys and taverns, in order to find out who had been sleeping with who, which brothels the Empire commanders frequented in the Ring, and to find out which Empire commander was open to being paid off. Godfrey had deeper illicit contacts than most—indeed, he had spent his entire life accumulating them—and now they came in handy. It had also not hurt that he had paid each of his contacts off well. Finally, he had put his daddy's gold to good use.

Still, Godfrey had not been sure if they were reliable, not until the last moment. There was no one to sell you out like a thief, and he'd had to take the chance that he was being had. He knew it was a coin toss, and that these people were only as reliable as the gold they were paid. But he'd paid them with very, very fine gold, and they turned out to be more reliable than he thought.

Of course, he had no idea how long this division of Empire troops would remain loyal. But at least they had wormed their way out of one battle, and for now, had them at their side.

"I was wrong about you," came a voice.

Godfrey turned to see the Silesian general coming up beside him with a look of admiration.

"I doubted you, I must admit," he continued. "I apologize. I could not have imagined the plan you had up your sleeve. It was ingenious. I won't question you again."

Godfrey smiled back, feeling vindicated. All of the generals, all of the military types, had doubted him his whole life. In his father's court, a court of warriors, he had always been looked upon with disdain. Now, finally, they were seeing that he, in his own way, could be as competent as them.

"Don't worry," Godfrey said. "I question myself. I am learning as I go. I am not a commander, and I have no master plan other than to survive any way I can."

"And where to now?" the general asked.

"To join with Kendrick, Erec and the others, and do what we can to abet their cause."

They rode, the thousands of them, an awkward and uneasy alliance between the Empire men and Godfrey's, charging up and down hills, across long, dry dusty plains, heading to the valley where Kendrick had told them to rendezvous. As they rode, a million thoughts raced through Godfrey's mind. He wondered how Kendrick and Erec had fared; he wondered how outnumbered they would be; and he wondered how he would fare in the next battle, a *real* battle. There was no more avoiding it; he had no more tricks up his sleeve, no more gold.

He gulped, nervous. He felt that he did not have the same level of courage that all the others seemed to have, that they all seemed to be born with. Everyone else seemed so fearless in battle, and even if life. But Godfrey had to admit he was afraid. When it came down to it, to the thick of battle, he knew he would not shirk. But he was clumsy and awkward; he did not have the skills of the others, and he just didn't know how many times he would be saved by the gods of luck. The others didn't seem to care if they died—they all seemed too willing to give their lives for glory. Godfrey appreciated glory. But he loved life more. He loved his ale, and loved his food, and even now, he felt a growling in his stomach, an urge to be back in the safety of a tavern somewhere. A life of battle was just not for him.

But Godfrey thought of Thor, out there somewhere, captive; he thought of all his kin fighting for the cause, and he knew this was where his honor, as sullied as it might be, compelled him to be.

They rode and rode and finally, they all crested a peak and were afforded a sweeping view of the valley spread out below. They all came to a halt, and Godfrey squinted into the blinding sun, trying to adjust, to make sense of the sight before him. He raised one hand to shield his eyes and looked out, confused.

Then, to his dread, all became clear. Godfrey's heart stopped: down below, thousands of Kendrick's and Erec's and Srog's men were being dragged away, bound as captives. This was the fighting force he was supposed to meet up with. They were completely surrounded, by ten times as many Empire soldiers. They were on foot, wrists bound, all taken prisoner, all being led away. Godfrey knew that Kendrick and Erec would never surrender unless there had been good reason. It looked as if they had been set up.

Godfrey froze, struck with panic. He wondered how this could have happened. He had been expecting to find them all in the heat of a well-matched battle, had expected to charge in and join forces with them. But now, instead, they were disappearing into the horizon, already a good half-day's ride away.

The Empire general rode up beside Godfrey and scoffed.

"It seems your men have lost," the Empire general said. "That wasn't part of our deal."

Godfrey turned to him, and saw how anxious the general seemed to be.

"I paid you well," Godfrey said, nervous but mustering his most confident voice as he felt his deal falling apart. "And you promised to join me in my cause."

But the Empire general shook his head.

"I promised to join you in battle—not on a suicide mission. My few thousand men will not go up against an entire battalion of Andronicus'. Our deal has changed. You can fight them on your own—and I'm keeping your gold."

The Empire general turned and screamed as he kicked his horse and took off in the other direction, his men following on his heels. They soon disappeared down on the other side of the valley.

"He has our gold!" Akorth said. "Should we pursue him?"

Godfrey shook his head as he watched them ride off.

"And what good would that do? Gold is gold. I'm not going to risk our lives for it. Let him go. There is always more."

Godfrey turned and watched the horizon, the disappearing group of Kendrick and Erec's men, which he cared more about. Now he was without backup, and was even more isolated then before. He felt his plans crumbling all around him.

"Now what?" Fulton asked.

Godfrey shrugged.

"I have no idea," he said.

"You're not supposed to say that," Fulton said. "You're a commander now."

But Godfrey merely shrugged again. "I speak the truth."

"This warrior stuff is hard," Akorth said, scratching his belly as he removed his helmet. "It doesn't seem to quite work out as you expect it, does it?"

Godfrey sat there on his horse, shaking his head, pondering what to do. He'd been dealt a hand he had not expected, and he had no contingency plan.

"Should we turn back?" Fulton asked.

"No," Godfrey heard himself say, surprising even himself.

The others turned and looked at him, shocked. Others huddled closer to hear his command.

"I may not be a great warrior," Godfrey said, "but those are my brothers out there. They are being taken away. We cannot turn back. Even if it means our deaths."

"Are you mad?" the Silesian general asked. "All of those fine warriors of the Silver, of the MacGils, of the Silesians—*all* of them, and they could not fight back the Empire's men. How do you think a few thousand of our men, under *your* command, will do it?"

Godfrey turned to him, annoyed. He was tired of being doubted.

"I never said we would win," he countered. "I say only that it is the right thing to do. I will not abandon them. Now if you want to turn around and go home, feel free. I will attack them myself."

"You are an inexperienced commander," he said, scowling. "You don't know of what you speak. You will lead all these men to certain death."

"I am," Godfrey said. "That is true. But you promised not to doubt me again. And I won't be turning around."

Godfrey rode several feet out in front and up an elevation, so that he could be seen by all his men.

"MEN!" he called out, his voice booming. "I know you don't know me as a tried and true commander, as you do Kendrick or Erec or Srog. And it is true, I do not have their skills. But I have heart, at least on occasion. And so do you. What I know is that those are our brothers out there, captured. And I myself would rather not live than live to see them taken away before our eyes, than go back home like dogs to our cities and await the Empire to come and kill us, too. Be sure of it: they will kill us, too, one day. We can all go down now, on our feet, fighting, chasing the enemy, as free men. Or we can go down in shame and dishonor. The choice is yours. Ride with me, and live or not, you will ride to glory!"

There came a shout from his men, one so enthusiastic that it surprised Godfrey. They all raised their swords high into the air, and it gave him courage.

It also made Godfrey realize the reality of what he just said. He had not really thought through his words before saying them; he just got swept up in the moment. Now he realized he was committed to it, and he was a little shocked by his own words. His own bravery was daunting to even him.

As the men pranced on the horses, preparing their arms, getting ready for their final charge, Akorth and Fulton came up alongside him.

"Drink?" Akorth asked.

Godfrey looked down and saw him reaching out with a sack of wine and he snatched it from Akorth's hand; he threw his head back and drank and drank, until he nearly drank the whole thing, barely stopping to catch his breath. Finally, Godfrey wiped the back of his mouth and handed it back.

What have I done? he wondered. He had committed himself, and the others, to a battle he could not win. Had he been thinking clearly?

"I didn't think you had it in you," Akorth said, patting him roughly on the back as he belched. "Quite a speech. Better than theater!"

"We should have sold tickets!" Fulton chimed in.

"I guess you're not half wrong," Akorth said. "Better to die on our feet than on our backs."

"Although on our backs might not be half bad, if it's in a brothel bed," Fulton added.

"Hear hear!" Fulton said. "Or how about dying with a mug of ale in our arms and our head tilted back!"

"That would be fine indeed," Akorth said, drinking.

"But after a while I suppose, it would all get boring," Fulton said. "How many mugs can one man drink, how many women can one man bed?"

"Well, a lot, if you think about it rightly," Akorth said.

"Even so, I suppose it might be fun to die a different way. Not as boring."

Akorth sighed.

"Well, if we survive all this, at least it would give us cause to *really* have a drink. For once in our lives, we will have earned it!"

Godfrey turned away, trying to tune out Akorth and Fulton's perpetual banter. He needed to concentrate. The time had come for him to become a man, to leave behind witty banter and tavern jokes; to make *real* decisions that affected *real* men in the *real* world. He felt a heaviness about him; he could not help but wonder if this was as his father had felt. In some strange way, as much as he hated the man, he was beginning to sympathize with his father. And maybe even, to his own horror, to become like him.

Forgetting the danger before him, Godfrey was overcome with a surge of confidence. He suddenly kicked his horse and with a battle cry, raced headlong down the valley.

Behind him came the immediate battle cry of thousands, and their horses' steps filled his ears as they charged behind him.

Godfrey already felt light-headed, the wind in his hair, the wine going to his head, as he raced towards a certain death, and wondered what in the world he had gotten himself into.

CHAPTER FIVE

Thor sat atop his horse, his father at his side, McCloud on his other, and Rafi close by. Behind them sat tens of thousands of Empire soldiers, the main division of Andronicus' army, well-disciplined and patiently awaiting Andronicus' command. They all sat atop a ridge, looking up at the Highlands, their peaks covered in snow. Atop the Highlands sat the McCloud city, Highlandia, and Thor tensed up as he watched thousands of troops exit the city and ride towards them, preparing for battle.

These were not MacGil men; nor were they Empire soldiers. They wore an armor that Thor dimly recognized; but as he tightened his grip on his new sword's hilt, he was not sure exactly who they were, or why they were attacking.

"McClouds. My former men," McCloud explained to Andronicus. "All good McCloud soldiers. All men I once trained and fought with."

"But now they have turned against you," Andronicus observed. "They charge to battle you."

McCloud scowled, missing an eye, half his face branded with the Empire seal, looking grotesque.

"I am sorry, my lord," he said. "It is not my fault. It is the work of my boy, Bronson. He turned my own people against me. If it weren't for him, they would all be joining me right now in your great cause."

"It is not because of your boy," Andronicus corrected, steel in his voice, turning towards him. "It is because you are a weak commander and a weaker father. The failure in your boy is the failure in you. I should have known you'd be unable to control your own men. I should have killed you long ago."

McCloud gulped, nervous.

"My lord, you might also consider that they are not just fighting against me, but against you. They want to rid the Ring of the Empire."

Andronicus shook his head, fingering his necklace of shrunken heads.

"But you are on my side now," he said. "So to fight against me is to fight against you, too."

McCloud drew his sword, scowling down at the approaching army.

"I'll fight and kill each and every one of my own men," he declared.

"I know you will," Andronicus said. "If you don't, I will kill you myself. Not that I need your help. My men will do far more damage than you can ever dream—especially when led by my own son, Thornicus."

Thor sat there on his horse, dimly hearing all of their conversations, yet at the same time not hearing any of it. He was in a daze. His mind swarmed with foreign thoughts he did not recognize, thoughts that pulsated through his brain and continually reminded him of the allegiance he owed his father, of his duty to fight for the Empire, of his destiny as the son of Andronicus. The thoughts swirled in his mind relentlessly, and as much as he tried, he was unable to clear his mind, to think thoughts of his own. It was as if had been taken hostage within his own body.

As Andronicus spoke, each of his words became a suggestion in Thor's mind, then a command. Then somehow, they became his own thoughts. Thor struggled, some small part of him trying to rid his mind of these invasive thoughts, to reach a point of clarity. But the more he struggled, the harder it became.

As he sat there on his horse, watching the incoming army galloping across the plains, he felt the blood in his veins flowing, and all he could think of was his loyalty to his father, his need to crush anyone who stood in his father's way. Of his destiny to rule the Empire.

"Thornicus, did you hear me?" Andronicus prodded. "Are you prepared to prove yourself in battle for your father?"

"Yes, my father," Thor answered, staring straight ahead. "I battle anyone who battles you."

Andronicus smiled wide. He turned and faced his men.

"MEN!" he boomed. "The time has come to face the enemy, to rid the Ring of its surviving rebels once and for all. We shall begin with these McCloud men who dare defy us. Thornicus, my son, will lead us in battle. You will follow him as you would follow me. You will give your life for him as you would for me. Betrayal to him is betrayal to me!"

"THORNICUS!" Andronicus screamed.

"THORNICUS!" came the echo of the chorus of ten thousand Empire troops behind them.

Thor, emboldened, raised his new sword high, the sword of the Empire, the one his beloved father had given him. He felt a power welling through it, the power of his bloodline, of his people, of all that he was meant to be. Finally he was back home, back with his father, once again. For his father, Thor would do anything. Even throw himself to death.

Thor let out a great battle cry as he kicked his horse and went charging down the valley, the first in battle. Behind him came a great battle cry, as tens of thousands of men followed, all of them prepared to follow Thornicus to their deaths.

CHAPTER SIX

Mycoples sat curled up, tangled inside the immense Akron net, unable to stretch, to flap her wings. She sat at the helm of the Empire ship, and struggle as she did, she could not lift her chin, move her arms, expand her claws. She had never felt worse in her life, never felt such a lack of freedom, of strength. She was curled up in a ball, blinking slowly, despondent, more so for Thor than for herself.

Mycoples could sense Thor's energy, even from this great distance, even as her ship sailed across the sea, rolling up and down in the monstrous waves, her body rising and falling as waves crashed onto the deck. Mycoples could feel Thor changing, becoming someone else, not the man she once knew. Her heart broke. She could not help but feel as if somehow she had let him down. She tried to struggle once again, wanting so much to go to him, to save him. But she just could not break free.

A huge wave crashed on deck, and the foaming waters of the Tartuvian slipped beneath her net, making her slide, and banging her head on the wooden hull. She cowered and snarled, not having the spirit or strength that she used to. She was resigned to her new fate, knowing she was being taken away to be killed, or worse, to live a life in captivity. She didn't care what became of her. She just wanted Thor to be okay. And she wanted a chance, just one last chance, for vengeance on her attackers.

"There she is! Slipped halfway across the deck!" one of the Empire soldiers yelled out.

Mycoples felt a sudden jabbing pain on the sensitive scales of her face, and she saw two Empire soldiers, with spears thirty feet long, jabbing her at a safe distance through the net. She tried to lunge forward for them, but her constraints held her down. She snarled as they poked her again and again, laughing, clearly having fun.

"She's not so scary now, is she?" one asked the other.

The other laughed, jabbing his spear close to her eye. Mycoples moved away at the last second, sparing herself blindness.

"She's harmless as a fly," said one.

"I hear they're going to put her on display in the new Empire capitol."

"That's not what I heard," said the other. "I heard they're going to pry off her wings and torture her for all the harm she did our men."

"I wish I'd be there to see that."

"Do we really need to deliver her intact?" one asked.

"Orders."

"But I don't see why we can't at least maim her a little. After all, she doesn't really need both eyes, does she?"

The other laughed.

"Well now that you put it that way, I guess not," he answered. "Go for it. Have fun."

One of the men came closer and raised a spear high.

"Hold still now, little girl," the soldier said.

Mycoples flinched, helpless as the soldier came charging forward, preparing to plunge his long spear into her eye.

Suddenly, another wave crashed over the bow; the water took out the legs of the soldier, and he went sliding right for her face, eyes open wide in terror. In a huge burst of effort, Mycoples managed to lift one claw just high enough to allow the soldier to slip beneath her; as he did, she brought it down on him and pinned it through his throat.

He shrieked and blood spilled everywhere, mixing with water, as he died beneath her. Mycoples felt some small satisfaction.

The remaining Empire soldier turned and ran, screaming for help. Within moments, a dozen Empire soldiers approached, all bearing long spears.

"Kill the beast!" one of them screamed.

They all approached to kill her, and Mycoples felt certain that they would.

Mycoples felt a sudden rage burn through her, unlike anything she'd ever felt. She closed her eyes and prayed to God to give her one final burst of strength.

Slowly, she felt a great heat rise within her belly, travel down her throat, and she lifted her mouth and let out a roar. To her surprise, a slew of flames poured out.

The flames traveled through the net, and though not destroying the Akron net, still a wall of fire engulfed the dozen men coming at her.

They all shrieked as their bodies went up in flames; most collapsed on deck, and those that didn't die instantly ran and jumped overboard into the sea. Mycoples smiled.

Dozens more soldiers appeared, these wielding clubs, and Mycoples tried to summon the fire again.

But this time it did not work. God had answered her prayers, and had given her a one-time grace. But now, there was no more she could do. She was grateful, at least, for what she'd had.

Dozens of soldiers descended on her, beating her with clubs, and slowly, Mycoples felt herself sinking down, lower and lower, eyes closing in her head. She curled herself up tight, resigned, wondering if her time on this world had come to an end.

Soon, her world was filled with blackness.

CHAPTER SEVEN

Romulus stood at the helm of his massive ship, painted black and gold and waving the flag of the Empire, a lion with an eagle in its mouth, flapping boldly in the wind. He stood there with hands on hips, his wide muscular frame even wider, as if rooted to the deck, and stared out at the rolling, luminescent waves of the Ambrek. In the distance, just coming into view, was the shore of the Ring.

Finally.

Romulus' heart soared with anticipation as he laid eyes on the Ring for the first time. On his ship sailed his finest hand-picked men, several dozen of them, and behind them sailed thousands of the finest Empire ships there were. A vast flotilla, filling the sea, all sailing the banner of the Empire. They had sailed a long way, circling the Ring, determined to land on the McCloud side. Romulus planned to enter the Ring by himself, sneak up on his old boss, Andronicus, and assassinate him when he was least expecting it.

He smiled at the thought. Andronicus had no idea of the might or cunning of his number two in command, and he was about to learn the hard way. He never should have underestimated him.

Huge waves rolled past, and Romulus reveled in the cold spray on his face. In his arm he clutched the magical cloak he had obtained in the forest, and he felt it was going to work, was going to get him across the Canyon. He knew that when he put it on, he would be invisible, able to penetrate the shield, to cross into the Ring alone. His mission would require stealth and cunning and surprise. His men couldn't follow, of course, but he didn't need any of them: once he was in, he would find Andronicus's men—Empire men—and rally them to his cause. He would divide them and create his own army, his own civil war. After all, the Empire soldiers loved Romulus as much as they did Andronicus. He would use Andronicus' own men against him.

Romulus would then find a MacGil, bring him back across the Canyon, as the cloak demanded, and if the legend was true, the Shield would be destroyed. With the Shield down, he would summon all of his men, and his entire fleet would pour inside and they would all crush the Ring for good. Then, finally, Romulus would be sole ruler of the universe.

He breathed deep. He could almost taste it now. He had been fighting his entire life for this moment.

Romulus gazed up at the blood red sky, the second sun setting, a huge ball on the horizon, glowing a light blue this time of day. It was the time of day that Romulus prayed to his Gods, the God of the Land, the God of the Sea, the God of the Sky, the God of the Wind—and most of all, the God of War. He knew he needed to appease them all. He was prepared: he had brought many slaves to sacrifice, knowing their spilled blood would lend him power.

The waves crashed all around him as they neared shore. Romulus did not wait for the others to lower the ropes but rather leapt out off the hull as soon as the bow touched sand, falling a good twenty feet, and landing on his feet, up to his waist in the water. He didn't even flinch.

Romulus waltzed on shore as if he owned it, his footprints heavy in the sand. Behind him his men lowered the ropes and all began to filter off the ship, as one boat after another touched sand.

Romulus surveyed all of his work, and he smiled. The sky was growing dark, and he had reached shore at the perfect moment to present a sacrifice. He knew he had the Gods to thank for this.

He turned and faced his men.

"FIRE!" Romulus screamed out.

His men scurried to build a huge bonfire, fifteen feet high, a massive pile of wood ready, waiting to be lit, spread out and shaped in the form a three-pointed star.

Romulus nodded, and his men dragged forward a dozen slaves, bound to each other. They were tied up along the wood of the bonfire, their ropes secured to it. They stared back, wide-eyed with panic. They screamed and thrashed, terrified, seeing the torches at the ready and realizing they were about to be burned alive.

"NO!" one of them screamed. "Please! I beg you! Not this. Anything but this!"

Romulus ignored them. Instead, he turned his back on everyone, took several steps forward, opened his arms wide, and craned his neck up to the skies.

"OMARUS!" he cried out. "Give us the light to see! Accept my sacrifice tonight. Be with me on my journey into the Ring. Give me a sign. Let me know if I will succeed!"

Romulus lowered his hands, and as he did, his men rushed forward and threw their torches onto the wood.

Horrific screams rose up, as all the slaves were burned alive. Sparks flew out everywhere, as Romulus stood there, face aglow, watching the spectacle.

Romulus nodded, and his men brought forward an old woman, missing her eyes, her face wrinkled, her body curled up. Several of her men carried her forward in a chariot, and she leaned forward towards the flames. Romulus watched her, patient, awaiting her prophecy.

"You will succeed," she said. "Unless you see the suns converge."

Romulus smiled wide. Suns converge? That hadn't happened in a thousand years.

He was elated, a warm feeling flooding his chest. That was all he needed to hear. The Gods were with him.

Romulus grabbed his cloak, mounted his horse, and kicked it hard, beginning to gallop alone, across the sand, for the road that would lead to the Eastern Crossing, across the Canyon, and soon, into the very heart of the Ring itself.

CHAPTER EIGHT

Selese walked through the remnants of the battlefield, Illepra by her side, each of them going body to body, checking for signs of life. It had been a long, hard trek from Silesia, as the two of them stuck together, following the main body of the army and tending to the wounded and the dead. They forked off from the other healers and had become close friends, bonding through adversity. They naturally gravitated towards each other, each close in age, each resembling the other, and perhaps most importantly, each in love with a MacGil boy. Selese loved Reece, and Illepra, while she was loathe to admit it, loved Godfrey.

They had done their best to keep up with the main body of the army, weaving in and out of fields and forests and muddy roads, constantly combing for MacGil wounded. Unfortunately, finding them did not prove hard; they filled with landscape in abundance. In some cases, Selese was able to heal them; but in too many cases, the best she and Illepra could do was patch their wounds, put them out of pain with their elixirs, and allow them a peaceful passing.

It was heartbreaking for Selese. Having been a healer in a small town her whole life, she had never dealt with anything on this scale, or severity. She was used to handling minor scrapes and cuts and wounds, maybe the occasional Forsyth bite. But she was not used to such massive bloodshed and death, such severity of wounds and wounded. It saddened her profoundly.

In her profession, Selese yearned to heal people, and to see them well; yet ever since she had embarked from Silesia, she had seen nothing but an endless trail of blood. How could men do this to each other? These wounded were all sons to someone, fathers, husbands. How could mankind be so cruel?

Selese was even more heartbroken by her lack of ability to help each person she encountered. Her supplies were limited to what they could carry, and given their long trek, that wasn't much. The other healers of the kingdom were spread out, all over the Ring; they were an army in and of themselves, but they were stretched too thin, and supplies were too low. Without adequate wagons, horses, and a team of helpers, there was only so much she could carry.

Selese closed her eyes and breathed as she walked, seeing the faces of the wounded flash before her. Too many times she had tended a mortally wounded soldier crying out in pain, had watched his eyes glaze over, and given him Blatox. It was an effective painkiller, and an effective tranquilizer. But it would not heal a festering wound, or stop infection. Without all of her supplies, it was the best she could do. It made her want to cry and scream at the same time.

The two of them knelt, each over a wounded soldier, a few feet away from each other, each busy suturing a wound with a needle and thread. Selese had been forced to use this needle one too many times, and she wished she had a clean one. But she had no choice. The soldier cried out in pain as she stitched a long vertical wound in his bicep that did not seem to want to stay closed, continually seeping. Selese pressed one palm down, trying to staunch the blood.

But it was a losing battle. If only she had gotten to this soldier a day go, all would have been fine. But now, his arm was green. She was staving off the inevitable.

"You're going to be just fine," Selese said down to him.

"No I'm not," he said, staring up at her with a look of death. Selese had seen that look one too many times already. "Tell me. Will I die?"

Selese took a deep breath and held it. She did not know how to reply. She hated to be dishonest. But she could not bear to tell him.

"Our fates are in our maker's hands," she said. "It is never too late for any of us. Drink," she said, taking a small vial of Blatox from the satchel of potions at her waist, putting it to his lips and stroking his forehead.

His eyes rolled back, and he sighed, peaceful for the first time.

"I feel good," he said.

Moments later, his eyes closed.

Selese felt a tear roll down her cheek, and quickly wiped it away.

Illepra finished with her wounded, and they each got up, weary, and continued walking down the endless trail together, passing corpse after corpse. They headed, inevitably, east, following the main body of the army.

"Are we even doing anything here?" Selese finally asked, after a long silence.

"Of course," Illepra answered.

"It doesn't seem that way," Selese said. "We have saved so few, and lost so many."

"And what of those few?" Illepra countered. "Are they not worth anything?"

Selese thought.

"Of course they are," she said. "But what about the others?"

Selese closed her eyes and tried to imagine them; but they were just a blur faces now.

Illepra shook her head.

"You think in the wrong way. You are a dreamer. Too naïve. You cannot save everyone. We did not start this war. We only pick up after it."

They continued to walk in silence, trekking ever further east, past fields of bodies. Selese was happy, at least, for Illepra's company. They had provided each other company and solace, and had shared expertise and remedies along the way. Selese was astounded by Illepra's wide range of herbs, ones she had never encountered; Illepra, in turn, was continually surprised by the unique salves Selese had discovered in her small village. They complemented each other well.

As they marched, scanning the dead, once again, Selese's thoughts drifted to Reece. Despite everything all around her, she could not get him from her mind. She had traveled all the way to Silesia just to find him, to be with him. But the fates had split them apart too soon, this stupid war pulling them in two different directions. She wondered with every passing moment if Reece was safe. She wondered where, exactly, in the battlefield he was. And with each corpse she passed, she quickly glanced at the face with a sense of dread, hoping and praying it was not Reece. Her stomach clenched with each body she approached, until she turned it over and saw the face and saw it was not him. With each one, she sighed with relief.

Yet with every step she took she was on edge, always feared she would find him with the wounded—or worse, the dead. She did not know she could go on if she did.

She was determined to find him, dead or alive. She had journeyed this far, and she would not turn back until she knew his fate.

"I haven't seen any signs of Godfrey," Illepra said, kicking rocks as they went.

Illepra spoke of Godfrey intermittently ever since they'd left, and it was obvious she was smitten by him, too.

"Nor have I," Selese said.

It was a constant dialogue between the two of them, each smitten by the two brothers, Reece and Godfrey, two brothers who could not be more different from each other. Selese could not understand what Illepra saw in Godfrey, personally. He seemed to be just a drunkard to her, a silly man, not to be taken seriously. He was fun, and funny, and certainly witty. But he was not the vision of the man Selese wanted. Selese wanted a man who was sincere, earnest, intense. She yearned for a man who exhibited chivalry, honor. Reece was the one for her.

"I just don't know how he could have survived all this," Illepra said sadly.

"You love him, don't you?" Selese asked.

Illepra reddened and turned away.

"I never said anything about love," she said defensively. "I'm just concerned for him. He's just a friend."

Selese smiled.

"Is he? Then why do you not stop speaking of him?"

"Do I?" Illepra asked, surprised. "I hadn't realized it."

"Yes, constantly."

Illepra shrugged and grew silent.

"I guess he got under my skin somehow. He makes me so mad sometimes. I'm constantly dragging him from the taverns. He promises me, every time, that he will never return. But he always does. It's maddening, really. I'd thrash him if I could."

"Is that why you're so anxious to find him?" Selese asked. "To thrash him?"

Now it was Illepra's turn to smile.

"Perhaps not," she said. "Perhaps I want to give him a hug, too."

They rounded a hill and came upon a soldier, a Silesian. He lay beneath a tree, moaning, his leg clearly broken. Selese could see it from here, with her expert eye. Nearby, tied to the tree, were two horses.

They rushed to his side.

As Selese set to tending his wounds, a deep gash in his thigh, she could not help but ask what she had asked every soldier she had encountered:

"Have you seen any of the royal family?" she asked. "Have you seen Reece?"

All the other soldiers had turned and shaken their heads and looked away, and Selese was so used to disappointment that she by now expected a negative answer.

But, to her surprise, this soldier nodded in the affirmative.

"I have not ridden with him, but I have seen him, yes, my lady."

Selese's eyes widened with excitement and hope.

"Is he alive? Is he hurt? Do you know where he is?" she asked, her heart quickening, clutching the man's wrist.

He nodded.

"I do. He is on a special mission. To retrieve the Sword."

"What sword?"

"Why, the Destiny Sword."

She stared in awe. The Destiny Sword. The sword of legend.

"Where?" she asked, desperate. "Where is he?"

"He is gone to the Eastern Crossing."

The Eastern Crossing, Selese thought. That was far, so far. There was no way they could make it on foot. Not at this pace. And if Reece was there, surely he was in danger. Surely, he needed her.

As she finished caring for him, she looked over and noticed the two horses tied to the tree. Given this man's broken leg, there was no way he could ride them. The two horses here would be useless to him. And soon enough, they would die if they were not taken care of.

The soldier saw her eyeing them.

"Take them, lady," he offered. "I won't be needing them."

"But they are yours," she said.

"I can't ride them. Not like this. You'll put them to use. Take them, and find Reece. It's a long journey from here and you won't make it on foot. You've helped me greatly. I won't die here. I have food and water for three days. Men will come for me. Patrols come by here all the time. Take them and go."

Selese clasped his wrist, overflowing with gratitude. She turned to Illepra, determined.

"I must go and find Reece. I'm sorry. There are two horses here. You can take the other anywhere you need to go. I need to cross the Ring, to go to the Eastern crossing. I'm sorry. But I must leave you."

Selese mounted her horse, and was surprised as Illepra rushed forward and mounted the one beside her. Illepra reached out with her short sword and chopped the rope binding the horses to the tree.

She turned to Selese and smiled.

"Did you really think, after all we've been through, I would let you go alone?" she asked.

Selese smiled. "I guess not," she answered.

The two of them kicked their horses, and they took off, racing down the road, heading ever further east, somewhere, Selese prayed, towards   Reece.

CHAPTER NINE

Gwendolyn huddled low, lowering her chin against the wind and snow as she marched through an endless field of white, Alistair, Steffen and Aberthol beside her, Krohn at her feet. The five of them had been marching for hours, ever since they had crossed the Canyon and entered the Netherworld, and Gwen was exhausted. Her muscles ached, and her stomach hurt, sharp pains shooting through her every now and again as the baby moved. It was a world of white, snow falling relentlessly, whipping into her eyes, and the horizon offering no reprieve. There was nothing to break up the monotony of the landscape; Gwen felt as if she were walking to the very ends of the earth.

It had become even colder, too, and despite her furs, Gwendolyn felt the cold seeping into her bones. Her hands were already numb.

She looked over and saw the others shivering, too, all fighting against the cold, and she began to wonder if she had made a grave mistake to come here. Even if Argon were here, with no markers of any sort on the horizon, how could they ever find him? There was no trail, no path, and Gwen felt a sinking sense of desperation as she had no idea where they were all heading. All she knew was that they were heading away from the Canyon, ever farther north. Even if they found Argon, how could they ever free him? Could he even be freed?

Gwen felt as if she had journeyed to a place not meant for humans, a supernatural place meant for sorcerers and druids and mysterious forces of magic she did not understand. She felt as if she were trespassing.

Gwen felt another sharp pain in her stomach, and felt the baby turn within her again and again. This one was so intense she nearly lost her breath, and she stumbled for a moment.

She felt a reassuring hand grab her wrist and steady her.

"My lady, are you all right?" Steffen asked, quickly coming to her side.

Gwen closed her eyes, breathed deep, her eyes watery from the pain, and nodded back. She stopped a moment and placed a hand on her stomach and waited. Her baby clearly was not happy to be here. Neither was she.

Gwen stood there for a few moments, breathing deeply, until finally the pain passed. She wondered again if she had been wrong to venture here; but she thought of Thor, and her desire to save him trumped all else.

They began walking again, and as the pain subsided, Gwendolyn feared not only for her baby, but for the others, too. In these conditions, she did not know how long they could all last; she did not even know if they could turn back at this point. They were stuck. This was all uncharted territory, with no map, and no end in sight.

The sky was tinged with a purple light, everything tainted in amber and violet, making her feel even more disoriented. There was no sense of day or night here. Just an endless march into nothingness.

Aberthol had been right: this was truly another world, an abyss of snow and emptiness, the most desolate place she'd ever seen.

Gwendolyn paused for a moment to catch her breath and as she did, she felt a warm, reassuring hand on her stomach, and was surprised by the heat.

She turned to see Alistair standing beside her, laying a hand on her stomach, looking over at her with concern.

"You are with child," she said. It was more a statement than a question.

Gwendolyn stared back at her, shocked that she knew, especially as her stomach still looked flat. She no longer had the strength to keep it a secret, though, and she nodded yes.

Alistair nodded back knowingly.

"How did you know?" Gwen asked.

But Alistair merely closed her eyes and breathed deep, keeping her palm on Gwen's stomach. Gwen was comforted by the feeling, and felt a healing warmth spread through her.

"A very powerful child," Alistair said, her eyes still closed. "He's scared. But not sick. He will be fine. I am taking away his fears now."

Gwendolyn felt waves of light and heat rushing through her. Soon, she felt entirely restored.

Gwen was overwhelmed with gratitude and love for Alistair; she felt inexplicably close to her.

"I don't know how to thank you," Gwendolyn said as she stood up, feeling almost normal again, as Alistair removed her hand.

Alistair lowered her head humbly.

"There is nothing to thank me for," she answered. "It is what I do."

"You did not tell me you were pregnant, my lady," Aberthol said sternly. "If I knew, I would have never advised this trip."

"My lady, I had no idea," Steffen said.

Gwendolyn shrugged, superstitious, not wanting all this attention on her baby.

"And who is the father?" Aberthol asked.

Gwen felt a deep sense of ambivalence as she said the word:

"Thorgrin."

Gwen felt torn. She felt waves of guilt for what she had done to Thor, for how they had said goodbye; she also felt mixed feelings about the child's lineage. She pictured Andronicus' face, and she shuddered.

Aberthol nodded.

"A most excellent lineage," he said. "You carry a warrior inside you."

"My lady, I would give my life to protect your child," Steffen said.

Krohn walked up, leaned his head into her stomach, and licked it several times, whining.

Gwen was overwhelmed by their kindness, and she felt supported.

Suddenly, Krohn turned and surprised them all by snarling viciously. He took several steps forward, into the blinding snow, his hairs on-end. He peered into the snow, ignoring them.

Gwen and the others looked at each other, puzzled. Gwen peered into the snow but could see nothing. She had never heard Krohn snarl like that.

"What is it, Krohn?" she asked, nervous.

Krohn continued to snarl, inching forward, and Gwen, nervous, lowered her hand to the dagger at her waist, as the others laid their hands on their weapons, too.

They waited and watched.

Finally, out of the blinding snow there emerged a dozen creatures. They were terrifying, entirely white, with huge yellow eyes and four long, yellow fangs, larger than wolves. They were bigger than Krohn, and each had two heads, and long fangs, descending nearly a foot. They emitted a low, constant, vicious noise as they approached the group, spread out in a wide semi-circle.

"Lorks," Aberthol said with fear, stepping back.

Gwendolyn heard the distinctive ring of metal as saw Steffen drew his sword. Aberthol clutched his staff out before him with both hands, while Alistair stood there, staring, intense. Gwendolyn clutched her dagger and held it tight, prepared to lay down her life to defend her baby.

Krohn wasted no time: with a snarl, he charged forward and initiated the attack. He leapt into the air and sank his fangs into the throat of a Lork, and even though it was bigger, Krohn was determined, and he wrestled it down to the ground in a snarling match. The sounds were vicious as they rolled and rolled. Soon the snow stained red, and Gwen was relieved to see it was with the blood of the Lork, Krohn pinning it down, victorious.

The other lorks jumped into action. Two of them pounced on Krohn, while the others charged right for Gwendolyn and the others.

Steffen ran forward, swinging his sword down on a lork as it charged for Gwendolyn and managing to chop off one of its two heads. But that left him exposed, and the other lork pounced on him and sank its long fangs into Steffen's arm. Steffen screamed out, his blood squirting everywhere, as the creature pinned him down to the ground.

Gwendolyn stepped forward with her dagger and stabbed the lork in its back; it arched its back as it screamed out. It kept one set of fangs inside Steffen's arm, while with its other head it turned and snapped at Gwen. It arched back just enough for Steffen to break free, and as Gwen retreated, holding her dagger before her with shaking hands, Steffen retrieved his sword and chopped off its heads.

A lork set its sights on Alistair and charged; it leapt into the air and aimed to sink its fangs into her throat.

Alistair stood calmly in place, though, unfazed, and she raised one hand out in front of her; a yellow light emanated from her palm and flew through the air and struck the lork in its chest. It hovered there, frozen in midair, as Alistair held her arm out.

Finally, after several seconds floating in the air, the creature fell to her feet, harmlessly, dead.

A lork charged for Aberthol, and he raised his staff and struck it in the air, as he sidestepped out of its way. The lork immediately regained its feet, though, and leapt onto Aberthol's back.

Aberthol screamed as the lork sank its fangs into his shoulder and pinned him down, face-first, into the snow.

Gwendolyn turned to help, but Steffen beat her to it, drawing his bow and landing an arrow in the creature's jaws before it landed a fatal blow on the back of Aberthol's exposed neck.

Steffen then turned to fire at the two lorks pinning Krohn down, but a sudden gale of snow made firing impossible.

Gwendolyn ran for Krohn. She drew her dagger and stabbed a lork in its back, and Krohn leapt off and sank his fangs in the other lork's throat. Steffen rushed forward and stabbed the lork in its other face before it could kill Krohn.

Finally, the lorks were all dead. They all grew silent.

Krohn, covered in wounds, regained his feet and limped over to Gwendolyn. He licked her hand and then her stomach.

Gwendolyn, crying to see Krohn wounded and so touched by his loyalty, knelt down by his side and rubbed his fur, feeling all his wounds and seeing all the blood in her palms. Her heart broke. Alistair knelt beside Krohn, lay her hands on him, and as a soft yellow glow covered his body, he looked up at her, and licked her face. His wounds were healed.

Alistair helped Aberthol up, and he regained his feet shakily. The five of them, all rattled, turned and looked at each other, at the carnage, taking it all in. It had all happened so fast, Gwen could barely process it. It reminded her once again of the dangers of this place.

"My lady, look!" Steffen called out, excitement in his voice.

Gwen turned and looked at the horizon, and she saw a temporary lull in the snowstorm. Slowly, a small burst of sunshine emerged between the clouds, a glimmer of hope on the horizon.

As she watched, to her shock, there suddenly appeared, floating on the horizon, a rainbow, all its colors glowing in the air. It was unlike any rainbow Gwen had ever seen: instead of being shaped in an arc, it was shaped in a perfect circle, hollow on the middle, floating high in the sky.

It also illuminated the landscape, and for the first time, she had a glimpse of her surroundings.

"There," Gwen said. "Do you see that ridge? The wall of snow ends. We must make it there."

Invigorated, the group increased their pace.

They marched in unison, up a high ridge, Gwen breathing hard, each of them supporting each other as they nurtured their wounds.

Finally, Aberthol stopped.

"I can't go on," he said.

"You must," Gwen implored.

She came over, draped one arm around his, and helped him up the hill, as Alistair came over and helped with the other. If they could just reach the top of the ridge, Gwendolyn hoped all would become clear. Perhaps they would see Argon somewhere; or perhaps, at least, there would be some indicator, some sign to point the way.

They climbed and climbed, and finally, breathing hard, they reached the very top. Gwendolyn stood at the peak with the others and looked down below. She was shocked at what she saw.

There, spread out below her as far as the eye could see, was a view unlike any she had seen in her life. It was an endless valley, the sky above it a clear yellow and red, no more snow to be seen. Instead, beneath the sky was a sparkling, frozen landscape. It was like a frozen city, but instead of buildings were mounds of ice, all different shapes and sizes, each a different color—violets, blues, reds, pinks. All of it sparkled in the sun, a million flashes of light.

It was a frozen city, the most beautiful thing she had ever seen. It did not look real.

Gwen had no idea what it was, or where it led. But she felt a magical sheen over it, felt that time and place were trapped here.

And she knew, she just knew, that Argon was somewhere below.

CHAPTER TEN

Reece balanced on the edge of the cliff, pressed up against the stone, hands shaking, clutching on for dear life and looking down over his shoulder in horror as he watched Krog plummet past him, screaming and flailing into the mist. Reece's heart sank. Krog was surely dead. They had already lost one of their valued Legion members, and Reece could not help but feel that it was his fault; after all, he was the one who had lead the men down here.

Reece's hands and feet were shaking, and he wondered how much longer he himself could hold on—and how much longer the rest of the men could, too. He didn't feel like they could make it much longer—and he still didn't know if the bottom even existed. Had he been reckless to pursue this?

But suddenly there came a nice surprise—Krog's screams ended abruptly and were replaced with the sound of Krog impacting something. It sounded like branches, like twigs snapping, and it was all closer than Reece could have ever imagined. He was shocked: had Krog hit bottom? Was it so close?

Reece felt encouraged as he looked down into the swirling mist, knowing that Krog was not too far below. Maybe even, Reece hoped, he had lived. Maybe something had cushioned his fall.

"KROG!?" Reece called down.

There came no response.

Reece looked up and saw the others, Elden, O'Connor, Conven, Indra and Serna, all clinging to the side of the cliff, hands shaking, and all looking down with the same expression of shock and fear. Reece could tell from their bodies, from their desperate expressions, that they would not make it much farther either. He felt obliged to set an example as their leader.

"The bottom is close!" Reece called out, mustering confidence in his tone. "Krog hit it. He will be okay—and so will we! Hang on just a little bit more, and we will all be to safety. Follow me!"

Reece scurried down, hands slipping, knees shaking, but determined to make it and to set an example. When he thought only of himself, it felt too hard; but when he thought of others, he felt renewed energy.

Breathing hard, Reece looked below and focused. He just tried to make it from one foothold to the next; sometimes there was just enough room for his toes. His boots luckily gave him support, allowing him to cram his toes into tiny spots and lodge them there, and giving him the strength he needed to support his body. He scrambled down the cliff with his final burst of energy, praying to God that this was the end.

Finally, the swirling mist began to lift, and as Reece looked down, his heart soared to see land. Real land! Hardly twenty feet below, there was the canyon bottom.

And lying there, on a bed of what look liked soft pine needles, bright turquoise in color, lay Krog. He groaned and writhed on the floor. Reece sighed with relief. He was alive.

As he neared, Reece was shocked at the landscape down below: it was more exotic than anything he had ever seen, and it looked like he had arrived on another planet. He caught only glimpses of it between the swirling mists, but from what he could see, the canyon bottom was littered with pine trees, with bright orange trunks and bright turquoise needles, its branches were purple and gold and littered with exotic, small fruits that sparkled. The soil looked like mud.

As Reece reached the last few feet, he jumped down off the wall, his hands barely able to hold on one more second. His feet landed in the soil, and they sank a few inches. He looked down and saw a strange sticky substance, not quite mud, but not quite soil. It felt so good to have his feet on real ground again.

All around him, his fellow Legion followed his example, jumping down off the last few feet of wall and landing beside him.

Reece hurried to Krog's side. As he approached, a flash of anger burst through Reece: Krog had been a Thorn in his side the whole time. Yet despite that, Reece was determined not to treat Krog the same way he had been treated by him. He had to rise above that, and regardless of what Krog deserved, it was not leader-like to sink to his level. Petty revenge might be a way for boys—but not for men. And it was time for him to leave boyhood behind, and to become a man.

Reece knelt beside Krog and surveyed him, determined to help.

Krog groaned, squinting his eyes, writhing in pain.

"My knee," Krog gasped.

Reece looked down and winced as he saw a large, purple branch impaled through Krog's knee, through one side and out the other. Reece's stomach churned at the site; it looked beyond painful.

"How does it look?" Krog asked.

Reece forced himself to look back at Krog with a steady expression of calm and cool confidence, not wanting Krog to panic.

"I've seen worse," Reece responded. "You will be fine."

Krog, though, didn't seem to buy it. He was sweating, and looked up at him with panic stricken eyes. His breathing was rapid and shallow.

"Listen to me," Reece insisted, grabbing his cheeks. "Do you hear me? Your knee will be fine. Do you trust me?"

Slowly, Krog's breathing slowed, and he nodded back.

All the others appeared beside Reece, and they stopped short in their tracks, looking down. Reece was sure that they were looking down at Krog's knee with the same shock he had experienced.

"You're lucky you're alive," Serna said to him. "I was sure you were dead."

"The branches cushioned my fall," Krog said. "I think I broke half the tree."

Reece looked up and saw half the tree missing its branches.

Krog tried to move, but winced and shook his head.

"I can't bend my leg. I can't walk." Krog breathed sharply. "Leave me here," he said. "I'm useless to you now."

Reece shook his head.

"Do you remember our motto?" he reminded. "*No man left behind.* Those aren't empty words. We live by them. And we aren't leaving you anywhere."

Reece thought quick, and turned to the others.

"Elden, O'Connor, hold him down," he commanded, using the voice of authority.

They each knelt down and grabbed a shoulder, pinning Krog down.

"What are you doing?" Krog asked.

Reece didn't hesitate; he had to get it over with. He reached up, grabbed the branch protruding through his knee, snapped off on end of it, and then, as Krog let out a horrific scream, yanked it straight through the other side, until it was clear out of his leg. Blood gushed, and Reece reached down and stopped it up with his palm.

Krog flailed, moaning, and Indra rushed down beside him, tore a strip of cloth off the end of her shirt, and wrapped his wound.

"Son of a bitch!" Krog screamed, writhing in agony, digging his hands into Reece's forearm.

"You are going to be okay," Reece said. "Conven—your sack."

Conven rushed forward, lowered his sack of alcohol left over from Silesia, grabbed Krog's cheeks and squirted it down his throat. Krog struggled at first, but Conven held him firmly, forcing him to drink. Eventually Krog's eyes started to glaze over, his screaming quieted, and Reece knew that the strong drink was kicking in.

"Get him to his feet," Reece said, rising.

Elden and O'Connor dragged him to his feet, each draping an arm around one shoulder.

"I hate you," Krog, half delirious, moaned to Reece, glaring at him.

Reece shrugged. He never expected Krog to like him; he didn't help him for that reason.

"Hate me all you want," he said. "At least your leg will be saved."

Reece turned and surveyed his surroundings, taking it all in. He was surprised and disoriented to actually be down here. Everything felt so foreign, so exotic, as if he were worlds away from the Ring. They stood in the midst of a brightly-colored forest, the swirling mists rushing through. Large mounds of mud rose up here, dotting the landscape, looking like large disfigured boulders rising up from the earth. Springs of steam rose in various pockets from the bottom of the floor, hissing as they shot up into the air, stopping and starting abruptly with no rhyme or reason.

Everywhere the air was filled with strange noises, caws and coos and snarls and shrieks; it sounded as if they had been dropped in the center of an animal kingdom. Reece peered into the midst, trying to get a glance, but the persistent mist made it impossible to see past twenty feet, making the noises even more ominous.

He turned to the others, who all looked back at him in wonder.

"Where to now?" Serna asked.

They all looked to Reece, and it was clear they considered him their leader now. Reece was beginning to feel more like a leader himself, too.

"We must find the Sword," Reece answered, "and get out."

"But it could be anywhere," Elden said.

"We can't see more than a few feet in front of us," O'Connor added. "There are no trails, no markers. How are we to find it?"

Reece turned and surveyed the landscape, and realized they were all right. But that wasn't going to stop him from trying.

"Well, one thing I know for sure," he said. "We won't find it by standing here. Let's move."

"But where?" Indra asked.

Reece picked a direction and began to walk, and he heard the others falling in behind, drawing their swords, all panicky.

He wished he could tell them he knew where they were going. But the truth was, he had absolutely no idea.

CHAPTER ELEVEN

Kendrick, Erec, Bronson and Srog, wrists bound, led by ropes by their Empire captors, marched before their thousands of soldiers, all of them prisoners of war now. Kendrick seethed with rage and humiliation, and looked up at Tirus, who rode smugly side by side with the Empire commander. He vowed vengeance. Tirus had outwitted them, but he had done so through betrayal and treachery. Such a victory, in Kendrick's eyes, was no victory at all. He lacked honor. And Kendrick would rather have death than a stain on his honor.

Yet still, here they all were, MacGil's finest warriors, along with Bronson's McClouds, all of them now at this traitor's mercy, this lesser brother of Kendrick's father, who had aspired his whole life to bring down his family and usurp his father's throne. Tirus had found his opportunity with Andronicus' invasion. Knowing Andronicus, Kendrick knew that this could only end badly for Tirus. If only Tirus knew that, if only he could see the short-sightedness of his treachery.

Kendrick hated to surrender. Yet in Kendrick's view, this was not surrendering, but merely delaying. They would find another way, one day, somehow, to defeat them. Tirus had promised to treat them all with honor, as prisoners of war. Kendrick trusted him on this point; he did not imagine Tirus would sink so low as to sully whatever shred of honor he had left. If the war settled down, and Andronicus indeed allowed Tirus to control a portion of the Ring, Kendrick believed that Tirus would treat them fairly. Perhaps he would press them into his service. And one day, when Tirus least expected it, Kendrick would rally his men and rise up and defeat him.

Then again, if Andronicus betrayed Tirus, then anything could happen to Kendrick and his men. He remembered Silesia, their treatment at Andronicus' hand, all too well. Which is why Kendrick had his eyes open, alert to any possible moment for escape.

They had been marching for hours, and Kendrick had quietly discussed it more than once with Erec, Bronson and Srog, and they all agreed: they would escape, as long as they could free all their men.

"Where do you think they're taking us?" Bronson asked, beside Kendrick.

Kendrick looked out at the cold, desolate landscape before them. He saw in the distance a massive camp of Empire men, and in the center, a vast, empty area, fenced off. It looked like a holding pen. Kendrick realized that that was where they being brought.

"They will hold us here until Andronicus decides otherwise," Kendrick replied. "We are his trophies now."

"Unless Andronicus decides to have us killed," Erec added.

"But Tirus gave us his word," Bronson said.

"Tirus' word is not worth much," Srog chimed in.

"Did we make a mistake to surrender then?" Bronson asked.

Kendrick wondered the same thing.

"To fight while ambushed would have meant a certain death. At least now we have a chance."

Kendrick was yanked hard by an Empire soldier, and they all continued marching forward, heading towards the distant prison camp.

"Your wife sold us all out," Kendrick said to Bronson. "She is the one who tricked Thor into being captured at Andronicus' hand."

Bronson grimaced.

"You are right," he said, "she did. But Luanda is your sister, too. You know her nature as well as I."

Kendrick shook his head.

"My half-sister," he corrected. "Yet still, I recall her nature. Too ambitious. What did you see in her?"

Bronson shrugged.

"Our marriage was arranged—by our fathers. Your father. Nonetheless, I have to admit, I fell in love with her. Despite everything, she has a good side. Deep down, there is a good person in there. I guess, despite everything, I have to admit I still love her. I still have hope for her redemption."

"Love her?" Srog asked, mortified. "After her betrayal of us all?"

Bronson shrugged. He wished he could answer otherwise, but that was how he felt.

"I know she has done terrible things," he said. "But deep down, I know there is a part of her that is redeemable. She is too ambitious, and she has become the victim of her own flaws. But she can change."

Erec shook his head.

"And until she changes, how many of our men have to die?"

Bronson fell silent. Of course, they were right, and a part of him agreed with them. He wished he hated Luanda, wished he could just turn off his love for her. But he had to admit, a part of him still loved her, despite everything. He wondered if he would ever see her again, if she even cared for him anymore. He looked down and studied his missing hand, the stump that was there, and remembered that he'd lost it defending her, saving her from his father's wrath.

Had he lost if for nothing?

Finally, the huge group came to a stop as the Empire soldiers shepherded them into the fenced-off holding area. The Empire commander, high on his horse, Tirus beside him, looked down and faced off with Kendrick, Erec, Bronson and Srog. The camp fell silent as all the troops stopped and watched.

Kendrick and the others stood there and looked up, humbled, like common prisoners.

"Tonight, you and your men will stay in this prison camp," the general announced, his voice booming. "At dawn, you will be executed."

An outraged gasp spread throughout the MacGil camp, and Kendrick found himself gasping, too, shocked.

Tirus turned and looked at the Empire commander, looking surprised himself, his four sons beside him, prancing on their horses, looking equally disturbed.

"But my liege, that was not the deal we struck," Tirus said to the Empire commander. "These men were supposed to be *my* prisoners of war to do with as I wished. You promised no harm would come to them."

The Empire commander turned and looked back at him.

"There are no deals to be struck with the Empire. I speak for Andronicus himself. You are lucky we have kept you alive. Unless you have changed your mind and you and your men would like to be killed along with them?"

Tirus reddened, then lowered his gaze down to the ground, looking embarrassed and caught off guard. He fell silent, though, clearly realizing the Empire had the upper hand.

Kendrick fumed. He had been so stupid to trust Tirus again, to agree to surrender. Looking back, he should have fought to the death back there. They would have all died, but at least they would have all died with honor, as warriors, on their feet.

"I will give you a choice," the Empire commander boomed, looking at Kendrick, Erec, Bronson and Srog. "We can either execute you—the leaders—or execute a hundred of your men instead, and let you live. Who dies? You or your men?"

Without hesitating, Kendrick, Erec, Bronson and Srog all, in unison, said proudly:

"We will die."

They all stood there proudly in the silence, staring back defiantly, not a moment of hesitation running through any of their minds.

The Empire commander nodded back at them with a look of respect.

"True warriors. I expected no less. Tonight, ponder your last night on earth. Tomorrow, be prepared to meet your maker."

∗

Erec, Kendrick, Bronson and Srog stood outside in the darkness of night in their own small holding pen, apart from the other prisoners, each bound to a post, hands and feet tied behind their backs, a few feet away from each other. The four of them were set apart from the others, set to be executed, while the main body of prisoners stood behind a massive fenced-in area, perhaps a hundred yards away. As Erec looked out at them, he took solace in the fact that at least his men would live.

Before they had been set apart, all throughout the night, thousands of their men had come up to them, imploring them to decline the offer, not to be executed on their behalf. Of course, Erec and the others, while touched by their offers, would not listen. They were men of honor, and if anyone had to die, they would sacrifice themselves. Erec had no regrets about that. His only regret was not having a chance to be unbound, to have his weapons drawn, to go down in a great clash of battle, as he had always dreamed he would.

But the series of betrayals had led him to this: Luanda had betrayed Thor; and Tirus had betrayed them. They had all been too trusting and now they would pay the price for it. It always astounded Erec that others did not share the same sense of honor as he. He, personally, would rather die than betray someone; for him, honor was more precious than life.

Erec stood there, bound to a post, Kendrick, Bronson and Srog close by, and stared up at the starlit night. Erec had never spent any time on the McCloud side of the highlands, and the stars appeared different from here. It was cold here, the ground hard and the temperature dropping, and a gale swept across the landscape and entered his bones. But he did not shiver. He looked up at the night, and contemplating his time on earth being over, he wondered about his one true love: Alistair. Would he ever see her again?

Erec was so proud when Alistair had told him she would accompany Gwendolyn to the Netherworld, to protect her. It was an honor befitting his wife-to-be, and it made him love her even more. But he also worried for her. Would she make it back from the Netherworld?

Knowing he would be executed in the morning, Erec realized he would never lay eyes on her again, and the thought pained him. It was his only regret; he would give anything for a chance to see her one last time.

Erec looked around and saw that the holding area was lightly guarded, with only two Empire soldiers standing guard. It made perfect sense: the Empire had no need for guards, given that the four of them were bound to posts, stripped of their arms, and their army was in its own separate prison. In the morning, they would all be dead anyway.

Erec struggled against his ropes again, trying to break free; but he had no room to wiggle, not even an inch. As he looked out at the night, he spotted something out of the corner of his eye, moving quickly. At first he thought he was seeing things, but as he looked more closely he spotted a lone figure moving in the blackness, slinking around the periphery of their fence.

Erec was confused, trying to figure out who he was and what he was doing. As he peered into the blackness he caught a better glimpse, as the figure moved for a moment beneath the torchlight: he saw the armor of Tirus' men, the royal crest of Tirus' family emblazoned on the breastplate.

Before Erec could make sense of it all, he watched the figure creep out of the darkness, slip up to the entrance of the gate, remove a dagger from his belt, and slice the throats of the two Empire soldiers standing guard. Two quick grunts cut through the night, as the Empire soldiers slumped to the floor, lifeless.

The figure cut the ropes, pulled back the fence, looked both ways furtively, making sure no one was watching, and then rushed forward right towards Erec, bloody dagger still in hand. Erec hissed, and Kendrick, Bronson and Srog turned and looked, too. Erec watched him approach, transfixed by the figure, wondering who he was and why he was here. Who had just killed those Empire soldiers? Why was he racing towards them? Was he coming to kill them, too?

The figure slipped behind him and suddenly sliced the ropes binding his feet and hands. Erec stumbled forward, grabbing his wrists, massaging them where the ropes had dug into them. Erec turned, amazed, as the man sliced through the ropes binding Kendrick, Bronson and Srog, too.

The four of them turned and faced him, as he raised his face plate.

The boy, hardly older than 16, stared back with piercing hazel eyes, his curly brown hair spilling out past his ears. He looked like Tirus. He had just risked his life to set them free and murder two Empire soldiers, and Erec could not understand why.

"Who are you?" Erec asked.

"I am Matus," he replied. "The youngest of four sons of the house of Tirus."

"Why have you freed us?" Kendrick asked.

Matus shook his head earnestly.

"I disagree with what my father has done," he replied. "It is okay for us MacGils to have our differences—but as warriors and as knights, we must honor our word. Honor is all we have, and despite what my father may do, I live and die by my word. My father gave you his word. And if he will not honor it, then I will. He promised to keep you as captives, not to have you killed, and I will rectify his wrongs. You are free. Take your men and go. Go quickly, before the light of dawn."

Erec watched, mouth open in disbelief.

"When your father wakes and finds us gone, he will surely blame you," Erec said.

Matus shrugged.

"I want you all to live. I remember you fondly," he said to Kendrick, "from our days as youths. I would like to see the Empire ousted, and the MacGils reunited once again, as they once were. I would like to see the Upper Isles retake their place within the Ring. I do not share my father's desire for the throne. Politics disgust me."

Erec nodded back with great respect.

"You are a warrior beyond your years," Erec said. "You have done yourself great honor on this night."

"We will never forget this," Kendrick said.

"No debt is necessary," Matus said. "Just take your men and go far from here. Go to the Upper Isles. Our castle sits empty now. You will be safe there from Andronicus' reach."

Kendrick was touched by his offer, but he shook his head slowly.

"You are of a true and noble blood," Kendrick said. "I do remember you, very well. You were different than the others, different than your father. The blood of my father runs in you. We cannot accept your offer, however."

"Why not?" Matus asked.

"Your isles may mean safety for us," Erec explained, "but that is not what we were born to do. We were born to fight, not to hide, and fight we shall."

"But you cannot win," Matus said.

"Perhaps not here," Kendrick said, "and perhaps not on this night. True, we stand outnumbered. But we will regroup, in some other place, on some other day, and fight then. Come, join our ranks."

Matus hesitated.

"Join us," Bronson added. "There can be no safe harbor for you here anymore."

Matus shook his head.

"I have done what I've done," he said. "I have no regrets. I will face my father, and whatever punishment he decides, I will accept. That is my way. I do not run from anything either. Now go."

Erec, greatly impressed by this young warrior, stepped forward, looked him earnestly in the eye, and clasped forearms.

Kendrick, Bronson and Srog did the same.

"I hope to see you one day again, my cousin," Kendrick said.

Quickly, Erec, Kendrick, Bronson and Srog turned and fled through the night, grabbing the weapons of the felled soldiers, racing across the blackness, and towards their men. Erec was elated, his prayers answered. They would free their men, take their army, and live to fight another day.

CHAPTER TWELVE

Andronicus galloped across the plains, his son Thornicus at his side, his sorcerer Rafi on his other side, and McCloud behind him. Behind them followed tens of thousands of loyal Empire soldiers, all of them riding with enthusiasm for one destination: Highlandia, the highest city, built on the very peak of the Highlands. Andronicus could see it before him, sitting there on the horizon, shining in the early morning sun, the highest city in the Ring, striding the two sides of the Highlands, and the last stronghold of the McClouds. McCloud soldiers poured out of it, daring to face him. He could not wait to crush it.

Andronicus had expected the McClouds to all surrender when McCloud had; they would have, too, if it were not for that rabble-rouser, Bronson. He had swept through the McCloud side of the Ring and agitated his people, and now thousands of them were rallying once again against the Empire invasion. Andronicus had received numerous reports of their killing his men, and now he was determined to take Highlandia, and crush the McCloud resistance once and for all.

Taking Highlandia also served another purpose for him: once he had the high ground, he would have a strategic point at the top of the Highlands from which it would be a straight shot down the other side, right across to the Western Kingdom of the Ring, back again to Silesia, where he could wipe out anyone left of the MacGils and crush the Ring for good. He smiled at the thought. He would take great delight in doing it—even more so, this time, with his own, Thornicus, leading the charge and slaughtering his own people. There was nothing Andronicus loved more than watching people murder their own. Which was why he was having McCloud lead this charge.

As much as Andronicus disliked him, he had to have Rafi ride upfront with them, too; he needed Rafi's dark energy close, needed Rafi to keep up his spells and to keep Thor under his mind control. He had also promised Rafi a reward: after the battle, Rafi would be allowed to gorge on the dead. Rafi loved to drink corpses' blood, and as much as it sickened Andronicus, he had to let Rafi have his way from time to time.

The group let out a great battle cry as they neared their target. They all galloped straight up the hill, rising into the sky as the McCloud army charged down to meet them. As Andronicus watched, he was surprised to see his son, Thornicus, charge out in front, farther than all the others, leading the pack. He rode and rode, faster, fearless, the first in battle by a good hundred yards. It looked as if Thornicus was going to challenge the entire McCloud army by himself. Thornicus was a thing of beauty to watch, all warrior, one hundred percent heart. He looked mythical, like a God on a horse, as if nothing in the world could stop him.

From out of Highlandia there came a great cry, as thousands of McCloud soldiers poured out, racing on their horses downhill, coming to meet the Empire army. They must have known they were outnumbered, yet still, these McClouds could do a lot of damage; given their strategic position, they could take out thousands of Empire men. They were probably gambling that Andronicus would not want to risk the loss of life.

But they did not know the Great Andronicus. He cared not for loss of life. In fact, he loved bloodshed, and he did not care how many of his men died. They were all just pawns to him anyway.

Thor was the first to meet the men in battle. Andronicus' heart warmed to witness this first true test of his son's fealty, to see if he would truly shed blood of his behalf. Thor cut through the McCloud army all alone, slicing and slashing every which way, creating a path of devastation that no one could touch. He was a one-man wave of destruction. McCloud was close behind, meeting his old army with a clash of arms, killing men left and right, equally gratifying to watch. He was Andronicus' toy-thing now, to do whatever Andronicus commanded, and there he was, killing his own people, people he'd once ruled, all for the name of the Empire. All for the name of the Great Andronicus.

Andronicus' army caught up, and the clash of arms rose to the heavens, greater and greater, the riding come to a standstill and his men fighting hand-to-hand. It was a vicious battle, bodies falling in both directions; the McClouds had down-hill momentum, and they used it wisely, taking out many of Andronicus's men, who were just too slow charging uphill.

Andronicus himself jumped into the fray, twice as tall as any man, swinging left and right. He did not flinch. He chopped off heads with single strokes, watching as they rolled to the ground, and wondering which to choose for his necklace. He pulled back his sword as a soldier approached, stabbed him in the gut and raised him high overhead, as if he were a piece of meat on a toothpick. He then pulled back the sword and stabbed another soldier in the gut, and hurled the two bodies into the crowd.

Rafi, not far from him, leapt from his horse and sank his yellow fangs into a soldier's throat, pinning him to the ground; he lay on top of him, sucking his blood. Other soldiers tried to attack him, but Rafi cast a spell, and there was a green light around him, and no one was able to come anywhere close.

The battle came to a standstill, thick with men, as the tide pushed back and forth. For a moment Andronicus was not sure which way it would sway—when suddenly, he saw Thor circle around and attack the McClouds from the rear, all by himself. He was such a force of destruction, so fast and strong and quick, that the entire rear flank of the army had to turn to fight him.

That freed up Andronicus' men to charge forward with a great cry. They slaughtered men left and right, finally breaking the back of the battle. They soon gained the momentum they needed, and they all finished their charge for Highlandia.

Those that remained of McCloud's men turned and fled, running for their lives. Thor stood in the middle, victorious, killing them every which way.

Andronicus rode to his son, meeting him in the middle of the battlefield, and he raised his sword proudly, facing him.

"Thornicus!" Andronicus yelled out.

"THORNICUS!" shouted his men behind him.

*

Andronicus paraded slowly through the vanquished streets of Highlandia, reveling in his victory. Thornicus rode at his side, surveying the damage with him. Andronicus watched with satisfaction as McCloud murdered the wounded, going from one to the next, as Andronicus had ordered him to do. The sound of steel piercing flesh cut through the air, as McCloud raised his lance high and leaned down on his horse and stabbed one wounded after the next, all his former people.

Andronicus smiled, taking it all in. There was nothing he loved more than a field of carnage. McCloud was totally in his power now, and he just loved watching someone torture his own people.

The ground was littered with corpses as far as the eye could see, and Rafi, flanked by his two henchmen, jumped from one to the next, as quick as light, kneeling and sinking his fangs into their throats, drinking until their blood dried out. He lay hunched over one now, his body quivering with delight as he gorged and gorged. He would be full tonight.

Finally, the tide had turned in Andronicus' favor. Nothing could stop him now.

Thor followed as they rode, father and son together, dozens of generals behind them. They rode to the very highest point of the city, at the edge of the mountains, and as they reached it, they stopped and looked down. Spread out below them, as far as the eye could see, sat the Western Kingdom of the Ring. Cutting through it was a wide road, disappearing into the horizon, the main road to Silesia. Andronicus could not wait to lead his army down that road. He was particularly excited to watch Thornicus kill his own people; nothing would give him greater joy.

But it had been a long day of battle, and with the sun setting, Andronicus decided it would be best to camp here for the night, and march in the morning.

"I have been looking for you everywhere," came a woman's voice.

Andronicus spun to see that annoying McCloud girl appear before him, Luanda.

He turned and frowned at her.

"Have you?" he asked.

"We will be entering the Western Kingdom soon. *My* territory. You promised, in return for my bringing you Thor, that it would be mine. So as soon as the battle settles, I have come to make sure you make all the proper arrangements to secure me King's Court and make me queen."

Andronicus stared back, in shock at her audacity. Then, finally, he threw his head back and roared with laughter. He could not stop laughing, especially as her haughty expression morphed to one of bafflement, then to embarrassment.

Luanda frowned.

"And what is so funny?" she asked. "Remember, you are addressing the daughter of a King, and a soon to be Queen."

Andronicus dismounted from his horse, and walked slowly towards her, the air thick with tension. He came up beside her, grabbed her by the shirt with one hand, and with one motion threw her from her horse.

Luanda screamed as she fell through the air, rolling to the ground covered in dust and dirt.

Andronicus reached down, grabbed her by her hair and tore a big clump off her head.

Luanda shrieked, and Andronicus raised the clump of hair high overhead, smiling.

"You're lucky your head is too small," he said, "or I would add it to my necklace."

Andronicus turned to his men.

"Arrest her, shave off the rest of her hair, and parade her through the camp for the entertainment of the men."

Luanda screamed, shaking.

"NO! You can't do this! You promised! You *promised!*"

They dragged her away, kicking and screaming, and Andronicus watched in delight.

No sooner had she left his view then there appeared before him that traitorous MacGil, Tirus. He approached Andronicus, his four sons beside him and dozens of soldiers in tow.

Tirus, at least, had the good sense to dismount, take a knee, and bow down to the ground before addressing the Great Andronicus, as did his sons.

"And what news do you bring me?" Andronicus asked. "Are Kendrick, Erec, Bronson and Srog all detained? Have you executed them yet?"

Tirus cleared his throat as he looked up, flustered.

"My Lord, I have delivered them all to you as promised, and your men have won the battle. But I am afraid I bear bad news."

"News?" Andronicus asked. He did not like the sound of this.

"Well..." Tirus began, "somehow...um...well.... They were our prisoners, but somehow...they escaped in the night. I'm sorry. I don't know how it happened."

Andronicus grimaced; he could feel a mounting fury rise up within him.

"Don't know how it happened?" he asked, incredulous.

"My liege," said the Empire commander, who came and knelt before him. "My men reported that they witnessed the MacGil leaders being freed in the night—by one of Tirus' sons."

Andronicus turned his gaze down to Tirus' four sons, kneeling there, all ashen with fear.

"It is not true, my lord!" Tirus yelled out. "My boys would never do such a thing!"

Andronicus, ignoring Tirus, stepped forward and examined each one. He saw something special in the piercing hazel eyes of the youngest; he detected the spirit of a warrior in him.

"You have taken something precious from me," Andronicus said to Tirus. "So I will take something precious from you. One of your sons will do."

Tirus looked up in shock and fear.

"My liege?" he muttered.

"Choose which one of your sons will die today," Andronicus ordered Tirus.

There came the ring of metal as Tirus drew his sword and began to charge for Andronicus, to defend his boys.

But Andronicus was much faster; he lunged forward and grabbed Tirus by the throat, and held him high overhead, with a single hand. Tirus was not a small man, and yet Andronicus handled him like a ragdoll.

Tirus dangled there, red-faced, gasping, as Andronicus held him up, dangling for all to see.

"If one of us is to die, then kill *me* my Lord!" cried out one of Tirus' sons.

Andronicus turned to see one of his sons, the one with the hazel eyes and curly hair, stepping forward and standing there proudly.

Andronicus dropped Tirus to the ground, and Tirus, gagging and coughing, curled up in a ball, clutching his throat.

"No, kill *me*, my Lord!" said another son.

"Take *my* life!" said the other.

The three brothers all stood forward, each asking to be killed over the other. Andronicus smiled as he debated which one he wanted to kill.

"You offered first," Andronicus said, as he approached the boy with the eyes.

Andronicus suddenly drew his sword, took a step forward and in a single motion, chopped off the head of Tirus' other son, the one standing next to the one with the eyes.

The other sons shrieked in dismay and Andronicus smiled.

"But you should know that I never kill the man who offers first."

CHAPTER THIRTEEN

Romulus charged down the dusty road as the sun rose, a dozen of his soldiers following, making his way across the desert, riding for the Canyon. He clutched his cloak as they rode, anxious to put it to the test.

The sacrifice of the night before had been a successful one, and Romulus felt satisfied that he'd appeased the God of War. He would cross the Canyon, that much he knew. His heart thumped with excitement as he imagined Andronicus' expression when he would see Romulus, inside the Ring, putting a sword through his spine.

The Eastern Crossing finally came into view, a bridge spanning a vast canyon, a great divide in the earth, greater than anything Romulus had ever seen. Swirling mist rose up all around it, lit up different colors in the early morning sun.

Romulus and his men dismounted as they reached the edge, and he walked to the precipice and stared down, hands on his hips, breathing hard from the ride. He knew that only he could cross with the cloak, but just in case somehow the Shield was down, he wanted these men to accompany him. The main body of his army he had left back at the shore. His plan was to enter the Ring, to find a MacGil, to get him back across the Canyon, to lower the Shield, and then to have his entire army invade.

In the meantime, he had these few men with him as a test, to see if by some chance the Shield was down. He knew it would risk their lives to try, but he cared not for the value of life. He would gladly sacrifice any of his men to fulfill his experiment.

"You," Romulus said, pointing to one of his men.

The soldier's eyes opened wide in fear as he realized. Still, he was quick to obey. He dismounted from his horse and walked alongside Romulus, and the two of them walked out in front of all the others, approaching the entrance to the Canyon bridge.

As they reached the threshold, Romulus stopped.

The soldier stopped, turned and looked at Romulus with a look of fear. He swallowed hard, then closed his eyes and braced himself, raising his arms to protect his face as he walked toward the bridge.

Suddenly, the soldier let out a horrific scream as his body melted, then turned to ashes, dropping in a pile at Romulus' feet.

The other men all gasped.

So, the Shield was still up.

Romulus draped the cloak about his shoulders and clutched it tight. He prayed that it worked. If it did not, he would end up like that pile at his feet.

Romulus breathed deep and took one big step onto the Canyon bridge. He braced himself, flinching.

His foot set down on the bridge, and Romulus was shocked: it worked. He had made it. He was standing safely on the bridge, wearing the cloak.

He continued to walk, farther and farther from his men, crossing ever deeper onto the bridge, alone. Soon, he would be inside the Ring.

*

Romulus rode on an Empire horse he'd found roaming the McCloud countryside, realizing it must have belonged to a slain Empire soldier left somewhere along the way. He been quick to find the horse once safely across the bridge and on the McCloud side of the Ring, and he'd ridden hard ever since, charging ever west, towards where Andronicus' main camp must be.

Romulus' first order of business was to ambush and kill his former boss, Andronicus—and for that he needed men.

He was not worried. The Empire's vast army feared and respected him as they did Andronicus—perhaps even more. Romulus was known to be an equally ruthless commander. He was also known to have the voice of Andronicus: anything Romulus commanded, the Empire men would assume came from the high commander himself.

Romulus was betting on his ability to convince the Empire men he encountered to follow him and join his cause. He would trick them, tell them that he had orders—from the Grand Council itself—to oust Andronicus. He would form a small army of his own, right here, inside the Ring, and would turn Andronicus' own men against him.

Romulus rode and rode, seeing the destruction all around him and realizing how many battles must have been fought up and down this land. It felt strange to actually be here, inside the Ring, this place he had heard of his entire life. He was so close, finally, to taking what was his, the rulership of the Empire forces. He felt as if he were riding into destiny.

Romulus crested the top of a ridge and looked down and saw below, a division of Empire, several thousand men milling about. This division was too small to be Andronicus' main camp; it must have been a vanguard, left to guard the rear. Andronicus saw the Empire banners waving, and his heart quickened as he recognized their commander.

Romulus kicked his horse and galloped across the countryside, riding down the gentle slope, not even slowing as he rode past the astonished looks of all the Empire soldiers, who stopped what they were doing, stiffened to attention, and saluted him up and down the ranks.

They parted ways, and Romulus charged right for the commander. He knew he would have to project his best authority to convince them to join his cause, and kill Andronicus.

As Romulus came to a stop, the commander wheeled, startled, fear in his eyes, and he jumped down from his horse, along with all his men around, and took a knee before Romulus.

"Sir, I had no idea you were coming," he said. "I would have arranged a parade in your honor."

Romulus dismounted, scowling, and strutted over to him. Romulus' reputation was well-known for killing commanders randomly, with no rhyme or reason, and this general trembled at the sight of him.

Romulus stopped but a foot away and boomed: "I've been sent by the Grand Council. A decree has been set. Andronicus is to be killed and I have been named the new Supreme Commander of the Empire forces."

The general stared back, his mouth dropped open in shock. Romulus would not give him time to process it.

"Mobilize your men at once, and ride with me," Romulus added. "We ride to fight Andronicus' forces and to oust him together."

"But sir…" the general said, stumbling, clearly unsure what to do. "We never received any such orders. We cannot kill Andronicus…he is our commander!"

Romulus knew he had to take definitive action. He stepped forward, grabbed the general with both hands and yanked him in, pulling his chin so close to his that they were almost kissing. He scowled down, his face trembling with rage.

"I will say this once," Romulus growled. "I am Supreme Commander now. Address me any other way, and I will have you killed, and instill a new general in your place. Do you understand?"

The general gulped.

"Yes, Supreme Commander."

Romulus threw him down to the ground, then he turned and scanned the soldiers' faces; they all immediately looked away, everyone afraid to meet his gaze.

"FOLLOW ME!" Romulus screamed, as he mounted his horse and kicked it, charging down the road.

Within moments, he heard behind him the sound of a thousand horses, rushing to do his will. A great battle cry rose up, and Romulus smiled wide.

He had his army.

CHAPTER FOURTEEN

Gwendolyn stood atop the ridge of ice, staring down in wonder and disbelief at the fantasy land spread out beneath her. The world before her was a frozen wonderland, sparkling with every color, soft shades of purples and violets and pinks, a million points reflecting off of the small mounds of ice. It looked like the world a day after a snowstorm, frozen in silence and peace, everything shiny and perfectly still. It was vast and overwhelming, stretching as far as the eye could see, a desert of light and ice.

She sensed that Argon was down there somewhere, trapped, and she felt more of a burning desire to free him than ever.

Krohn whined beside her, and Gwen looked over and saw Alistair, Steffen and Aberthol, the five of them all shivering, frozen to the bone, weary from the journey. One lost all sense of time in this place, and Gwen felt as if they had been trekking in the Netherworld for years. While Gwen had hoped to see some sign of Argon when they crested the ridge, instead, there appeared yet another vast landscape before them. She had hoped their trek would end here; but now it seemed as if was just beginning.

"It is endless," Steffen observed, standing beside her, looking out.

"The Ice Mounds," Aberthol said, eyes wide in awe. "I never thought to lay eyes upon it in my lifetime."

"You know of it?" Gwen asked, surprised.

Aberthol nodded.

"A place of profound magic. A place frozen in time. A place even the gods will not venture. It is a place to trap men's souls. A place that defies magic."

"But what is this place, exactly?" Alistair asked, also looking out in wonder. "It is not a desert, nor is it a city. It seems like...nothingness."

"At least the snow and the wind has stopped," Steffen observed. "At least we can see clearly before us."

"It is not what it seems," Aberthol said. "It is a world of illusion."

"Is Argon here?" Gwendolyn asked him.

Aberthol slowly shook his head.

"There is no way of knowing."

"There is one way," Gwen replied. "We find out for ourselves."

Aberthol shook his head.

"Look beneath you. The decline is too steep. It is solid ice. We could never hike down that. And if we did, this place is too dangerous. We would never return. It was folly to come here, but we should cut our losses. We must turn back now."

"But there must be a way—" Gwendolyn began.

Before she could finish her words, there came a cracking noise, and the ground beneath her suddenly gave way.

All of them screamed as they fell on their backs and slid straight down the icy slope. Gwendolyn could barely breathe they were moving so fast, the world whizzing by her as they went sliding, the ice scraping her arms. With nothing to slow their descent, they slid hundreds of feet, gaining speed. Gwen flailed, reaching out to grab something, anything, to slow or stop the fall—but there was nothing. Beside her, Krohn stuck out all four paws, trying to stop himself, but he could not. He slid headfirst, with the rest of them, all of them flailing, helpless. She felt they were sliding downward to their deaths.

Gwen braced herself as they approached the bottom, heading for a wall of white. She raised her hands to her face, expecting to hit a wall of ice and be crushed by the impact.

Gwen screamed and gasped as she hit the wall; but to her immense relief, she did not feel pain. She only felt a soft, wet cold, immersing her entire body. Gwen realized they had slid into a mound not of ice but of snow, and had come out the other side. She was dazed, and freezing, her entire body covered in snow—but unhurt.

Gwendolyn sat there, shocked, at the bottom of the valley, and looked over, and saw the others were, stunned, too.

"Are you okay?" she asked Aberthol, who looked shaken.

Aberthol blinked several times, checked his body, and nodded back. She saw that Steffen and Alistair were okay too, and even Krohn was walking. It had been scary, but they had made it. Their decision had been made for them.

Slowly, each of them got to their knees, then to their feet. Gwendolyn turned and looked back up the slope, saw the steep ridge from which they had descended, and could hardly believe it. She could not possibly imagine climbing back up there.

"Well, it seems we're stuck," Steffen said.

"At least we found a way down," Alistair said.

Gwendolyn turned and looked at the landscape before her. Down here, the ice mounds seemed larger, more imposing. They were spread out, like a thousand camel humps dotting the landscape, each tinged with a different color. They sparkled, and were beautiful. This place was so exotic, and Gwen had no idea what to expect.

"Now where?" Steffen asked.

"There is no way but forward. We must take the path before us," Gwendolyn said.

"But there is no path," Aberthol said.

"Then we shall make our own," Gwen replied.

She set off, walking through the field of mounds, and the group followed. They all walked forward, between the mounds of ice, all of them on edge as they traversed the strange landscape.

As they entered deeper and deeper into this place, Gwendolyn felt an increasing sense of foreboding, and wondered again if this had all been a bad idea. Was Argon even down here? And if he was, would they ever find him?

The blinding wind and snow had stopped, and at least the sky was visible, and Gwendolyn was grateful for that. But she was covered in bruises and bumps, her entire body aching, and she felt cold to the bone, weary from marching. She did not know how much longer they could all last. Eventually, they would have to make camp, and try to light a fire in this godforsaken place. She did not know if it was possible, and she had visions of them all freezing to death, lost forever here in this valley of trapped souls.

She needed to shake these dark thoughts from her mind; she needed to distract herself somehow.

"Tell me a story," she said, turning to Steffen as they walked, through chattering teeth. She was desperate for something, anything, to take her mind off the cold, off thoughts of danger. Sometimes, she realized, stories could be just as nourishing as food, or water, or heat.

"A story, my lady?" Steffen asked, his teeth chattering, too.

Gwen nodded, too cold to get out the words.

"Anything," she said.

They continued walking in silence, their boots crunching on the ice, silent for so long that Gwen wondered if Steffen would ever reply.

Then, finally, Steffen began:

"When I was young," he said, "I yearned to be a warrior. Just like the other boys. Of course, it was not meant to be, given my body. They made fun of me. I did not have the body they had, the height, the strength, the looks—any of it. I did not fit the profile of the warrior, and they would not allow me a spot for training. So, instead, my parents decided I would be the servant for the family."

Steffen sighed.

"I served them all, and those years were hard. But they could not break my spirit. When a day was over, after I'd worked all day for everyone, after I'd served and cleaned up after them all, after everyone was asleep and there was nothing left to do, my parents could not control me then. I snuck outside, roamed the hills in the moonlight, and I fashioned a bow myself, out of the finest sticks I could find. The local carpenter, he was a good man; he was not mean to me like the others, and he taught me how to craft one. He was impressed by my work, and over time, he gave me better and better scraps from his shop, and I made better and better bows.

"Before long, I was crafting the finest bows in town, bows that even the carpenter himself could not make. I turned out that I had a talent. He gave me arrows, and I taught myself. I would practice every night under the moonlight, until I became the finest shot in our village—and soon, even in our region."

Steffen sighed.

"Of course, my family knew nothing of this. I couldn't tell them. They would make fun of me, or take it all away from me, because they never believed in me. But one day, my bow was discovered."

Steffen fell silent, frowning, looking down, and Gwen could see the story pained him. He continued in the silence, the ice crunching beneath their boots, and Gwen wondered if he would continue.

Finally, he raised his chin and looked out at the ice with glassy eyes, as if looking directly into his past.

"The bow was under my bed," Steffen continued, "and somehow, one of my brothers had found it. He had held it up and asked everyone whose it was, and they all looked to me. They accused me of stealing it. My mother dragged me to the local castle to have me put in the stocks—until the carpenter heard, and explained that I'd made it. My family was incredulous. They never thought I could make anything.

"My brothers took the bow from me, and they demanded that I prove it, to prove that I could use it. I was glad to oblige, but my brothers snatched it from me and insisted that they try first. They all fired clumsily at targets, missing. When they tired of it, they gave me a turn. With one shot, twice as far as they, I hit the target perfectly, the target they could not.

"My father, instead of applauding, fell into a rage. He stepped forward, took the bow, and snapped it over his knee. I can still remember the sound of that snap. It was like the sound of my heart snapping. It broke my heart, and it broke my spirit."

Steffen sighed and turned to Gwen.

"My spirit has been broken ever since, my lady. It was not until I met you, until you gave me a second chance at life, that I began to feel my spirit revived. It was not until I met you that I ever raised a bow again."

Gwendolyn felt a surge of emotion at his story, and it took her mind off the cold, off of her weariness, off of everything. She felt a burning sense of compassion for him, and also a sense of pride. She related to his story in some odd way—to his suffering, at least. She thought of her own suffering, at the hands of McCloud, of how she persevered, of how the spirit could always persevere. She thought of how people could take things from you, how they could do their best to break you. But they could never break you, not if you didn't let them. If you can just hang in there long enough, she realized, one day you will meet someone, even just one other person, who will see you for who you truly are, and who will restore your faith in mankind, and restore your spirit.

"Thank you," Gwendolyn said to him.

They continued walking, trudging ever deeper into this strange world, weaving in and out of the mounds of ice, when suddenly, Gwen detected motion. She stopped as she saw a sudden movement out of the corner of her eye, something slithering on the ice.

"Did you see that?" she asked the others.

The others stopped beside her, and they all stared out at the landscape, peering between the mounds.

"I did not see anything," Alistair said.

But suddenly Krohn started snarling, stepping forward, hairs on end, carefully, one foot at a time, and Gwen knew she was right, she *had* seen something. It was something long and white, and it had slithered between these mounds. For the first time down here, she looked around, and she felt afraid.

"Maybe you were seeing things—" Aberthol added, but then stopped speaking as another creature appeared, slithering between the mounds, coming right for them. It was a huge, white snake with three heads, one at each end of its body and a third in the center. The snake, U-shaped, slithered in a strange way.

Steffen drew his bow and Gwendolyn her dagger, as the snake came towards them. Krohn snarled, and began to charge.

Just as quickly, the snake slithered away, disappearing from view, heading in a different direction.

"What was it?" Gwen asked.

"I have no idea," Aberthol said.

"Whatever it was," Steffen added, "it did not look friendly."

Suddenly, there came another one. Then another.

Several of them slithered towards them—but then they all turned away, at the last moment, scattering in every direction. The sound of their scales sliding along the ice gave Gwen the chills.

"They're not attacking us," Alistair observed.

"It looks like they're scared of us," Steffen said.

"Or like they're running from something," Aberthol added.

"From what?" Gwen asked.

There came a sudden tremor, and Gwen stumbled, as the ground beneath her shook. At first, she was sure it was an earthquake.

But suddenly, a huge mound of ice before her shattered, and out from it there sprang an enormous monster, fifty feet high and just as wide, entirely white, made, it appeared, of ice. He had a spine in the front of his body, and each vertebrae had a glowing red eye on it. It had eyes running up and down its arms, too, and at the end of each finger, it had razor-sharp teeth, ten mouths, opening and closing, snapping as the fingers came towards them.

It took a step closer and the ground shook. Gwen stumbled as the monster lowered its teeth right for her, coming too fast. In a moment, she knew, she would be dead.

CHAPTER FIFTEEN

Reece draped one arm over Krog's shoulder, O'Connor supporting the other, the two of them helping him walk as the group hiked deeper into the unknown wilds of this exotic world at the base of the Canyon. Sunlight streamed in faintly through the turquoise and orange leaves of the strange trees that grew down here; Reece craned his neck and looked straight up, and through the swirling mists he saw the immensity of the Canyon walls, rising up into the sky, impossibly high. This place seemed magical. Reece could hardly conceive that they had come this far, had descended this deep, and he wondered if they would ever be able to make it back up again.

More importantly, as he surveyed their surroundings, he wondered if they would ever be able to find the Sword. There was no trail or marker, or anything to follow; the Sword could be anywhere. He marched through the mud-like material, a gooey substance sticking to his boots, this place filled with the sound of strange creatures. Reece had never imagined that there could be a whole world down here, plants and animal life, its own terrain, like a whole separate universe, sitting between the two sides of the Ring. He wondered what sort of creatures could live here, in the depths of the earth. He wondered if people could live down here, too.

"So now what?" O'Connor asked aloud the question burning on all of their minds, searching the exotic landscape for any signs of the Sword.

"We can't just wander down here forever," Serna said. "We have no idea where the Sword went."

"Think about it," Reece said, "it can't be far off. We scaled down the Canyon wall right at the base of the bridge—and the boulder plunged straight down beneath the bridge. As long as we stick closely to this area under the bridge crossing, we must run into it. All we have to do is traverse the Canyon from one side to the other."

"But I can't even see the bridge from here, can you?" Elden asked.

Reece looked up, as did the others, and through the swirling mists there was no longer any sign of the bridge.

"You're assuming that we climbed straight down," Indra said to Reece. "We didn't. We climbed down erratically, following footholds. We may not be under the bridge at all."

Reece felt a pit in his stomach as they continued, wondering if she was right. Perhaps his plan was a bad one, and they were farther from finding the Sword than he thought.

As they continued marching, slogging through the mud, there came a sudden, fierce roar, making the hair stand up on Reece's back. They all stopped in their tracks. They clutched the hilts of their swords, looking at each other, eyes open wide with fear.

"What was that?" Serna called out.

"Looks like we're not alone," Indra said, the first to draw her sword. The sound of the metal rang through the air with a distinctive ring.

The roar came again, shaking the ground with a great tremor. Reece's apprehension deepened; it sounded enormous, and very upset.

"Whatever it is," Elden observed, "it sounds like our weapons are not going to do us much good."

The roar came a third time, and they all took a step back, in different directions; they could not tell from which direction it was coming. They turned every which way, forming a loose circle.

As Reece watched the mist, there slowly emerged a huge, hideous beast. It was bright red, covered in thick scales, and stood on two feet, thirty feet tall, muscles bulging. Its long arms ended in snapping claws, like lobster claws, and its head was all mouth, one huge set of jaws, opening and closing, revealing rows and rows of razor-sharp teeth.

It leaned back its head and roared, its narrow eyes squinting in fury, and a long tongue protruded several feet from its mouth, then retracted.

Reece looked up in terror, and saw the others were panicked, too. He drew his sword, as did Elden, letting go of Krog, who stumbled, then sank to his knees. The others all drew their swords, too, while O'Connor drew his bow.

"It does not seem happy," Indra said wryly.

The beast roared again, took several steps forward, and faster than Reece could imagine, swung down one arm, smacking Reece in the ribs with its forearm and sending him airborne. He went flying through the air, crashing into a tree, taking out its branches, and tumbling end over end as he slammed down to the muddy ground.

Reece rolled to his side, ribs hurting, head ringing, and turned and looked back.

The monster was on a rampage, charging for the others with fury. O'Connor, to his credit, stood firm, managing to pull back his bow and fire several shots.

But the arrows bounced harmlessly off the beast's scales, falling to the ground. The beast then reached out with its snapping claws, and snapped O'Connor's bow in half. With its other claw, the beast aimed to slice O'Connor in half. O'Connor dodged out of the way— but not quickly enough. The beast sliced his arm, making him scream out in pain as blood went everywhere.

Indra did not back down either: she reached back and threw a dagger at the beast's head. Her aim was true, but the dagger merely bounced off the beast's head, which seemed to be made of some sort of armor. It turned and shrieked and came right for her, its claws opened wide, as it went to bite off her hand.

Elden rushed forward, raising his ax, and chopped the beast's wrist with all his might. The blow was strong enough to sway the claw, but its scales were so tough, even Elden's great axe blow could not sever it. Elden only exposed himself to the wrath of the beast. It spun and backhanded him, smashing them in his nose, breaking it, as Elden screamed out and landed flat on his back.

The beast, not satisfied, brought its other claw down, right for the exposed Elden.

Conven let out a battle cry, and charged forward with his sword, and plunged it into the beast's stomach. But the sword barely scratched it, and the beast swung around, and opened its jaw and clamped down on the sword, snapping it in two like a toothpick.

Reece shook off his blow, gained his feet, and sprinted for the beast, this time aiming for its exposed back. As it brought its claws down for Conven, about to sink them into his chest, Reece jumped onto the beast's back, and sunk his sword right into its spine.

Finally, Reece found a soft spot. The sword sunk in, up to the hilt, and the beast shrieked an awful sound. It reached back, grabbed Reece with its claw, picked him up high above his head, and threw him through the air.

Reece went flying again, hurling end over end, so fast he could hardly breathe, and smashed face-first into the mud. He was winded, and felt as if he'd cracked a rib.

Reece turned around, and looked up, bleary-eyed, as the beast approached him. He watched, helpless, as the beast raised its foot high and prepared to stop him to death. He saw the razor-sharp claws on the sole of its foot, saw all of his friends knocked out, unable to move, and as he watched the claws coming down right for his face, he knew that in moments, his life would be over.

His final thought was: *what an awful place to die.*

CHAPTER SIXTEEN

Thornicus sat on a small boat, drifting alone at sea, in unfamiliar territory. He looked all around, searching for anything familiar, but the landscape was utterly foreign. He felt that he was far from home, on the other side of the universe, and that he would never go back. He had never felt so alone in his life.

Thor leaned over the bow and looked down into the waters, and as he did, he saw a face staring back at him.

But it was not his face; instead, it was the face of his father.

Andronicus.

"Thornicus," came a voice.

Thor leaned back and looked up into the sun, as it broke through behind the clouds. He squinted and saw before him a huge cliff and at its peak, a castle, the sun shining behind it. A stone footbridge arched high in the sky, leading to it, twisting and turning, narrow. Thor reached up for it, but felt as if it were a world away.

"Thorgrin, come to me," came the woman's voice.

Thor raised one hand to the sun and saw, standing at the edge of the cliff, a woman, around which glowed a violet light. She held her hands out, palms at her sides, and he could feel her summoning him. He knew it was his mother.

"Mother," he said, standing, reaching out a hand for her, trying to make it.

"Thorgrin," she answered. "You are my son, too. It is up to you to claim your lineage. You can choose your father—or you can choose me. You are both of us. Don't forget. Neither one of us is stronger than the other. You have the power to choose. You don't have to choose your father. You are not your father. And you are not me. Come home. Come to your true home. I await you."

Thor tried to stand, but he felt himself stuck; he looked down and saw his legs were shackled, bound to the boat.

"Mother," he called out, his throat dry, his voice raspy. "I can't. I can't break free. Help me."

"Try," she said. "You have the strength. Do not be deceived: you have the strength."

Thor tried to break free with all his might. As he did, he heard a gradual splintering of wood. He felt rushing cold water on his feet, and he looked down to see a hole opening in the bottom of the boat.

He suddenly fell through it, plunging down, screaming, into the dark and freezing sea, engulfed by water, as he sank into the depths of the ocean.

Thor woke breathing hard. He sat upright and looked about, sweating, trying to collect himself. He saw soldiers sleeping on the ground all around him, but he did not recognize them. It was all so confusing: they were Empire soldiers. What was he doing with them?

A cold breeze came and Thor looked down and saw he was lying on the cold, hard ground, on pebbles and dirt, camped out with all the other soldiers. He still wore his armor, his boots, and as he sat up, he was beginning to realize it had been a dream. He was on dry land. And his mother was nowhere in sight.

Thor rubbed his head, his mind muddled, trying to gain clarity. He looked over and saw, not far away, Rafi, sitting up in the night, staring back at him, his yellow eyes glowing beneath his hood. Rafi chanted a strange tune, and Thor felt it invading his thoughts, entering his brain, making all free thought impossible. The incessant humming drowned it out. As he heard it, all Thor could think of was his obligation to his father. His obligation for loyalty to the Empire.

Thor jumped to his feet, his armor rankling, shaking his head, trying to understand. He looked out into the night and he saw the Ring. But this was not the Ring he knew. This was not his homeland. He was in a foreign part of the Ring. And as he looked out, he did not see this land anymore as home; instead, he saw it as a place to invade. A place that needed to be crushed.

Thor looked about: in the still night air all around him, thousands of Empire soldiers lay fast asleep, the embers of bonfires glowing. He was starting to feel clear again. He was Andronicus' son. He was heir to the Empire. And he owed his father a great debt.

Thor spotted a sudden movement out of the corner of his eye, the only motion in the black of night. He saw a lone soldier, slithering through the night, passing by rows of soldiers, and heading for the large tent just feet away.

Andronicus' tent.

Thor watched as the figure sprinted, holding something at his side. He looked closer and saw that it was long and sharp, and glistened beneath the torchlight. And that was when Thor realized: the man held a dagger. This man, sprinting towards the tent, creeping silently through the night, was an assassin. And he was aiming to kill Thor's father.

Thor jumped into action, sprinting across the camp, racing to stop the assassin.

The assassin sprinted up to the two soldiers standing guard and sliced both of their throats silently before either could say a word. They both slumped silently down, dead. He then rushed right through the flaps of Andronicus' tent.

Thor was just a few feet behind them, and he burst through the flaps on the assassin's heels. As he entered, Thor saw the assassin a foot before his father, raising the dagger high for his back. Andronicus lay there in his bed, on his stomach, unsuspecting; he had no idea he was about to be killed.

Thor burst into action: he reached to his waist, grabbed his sling, placed a stone, and hurled it with all his might.

The stone lodged itself in the back of the assassin's neck, embedding itself deeply. The assassin froze, his dagger high in the air, just inches away from Andronicus—then he slumped over and fell face-first to the ground beside him, his dagger falling harmlessly to his side.

Dead.

Andronicus jumped up, eyes wide with panic, and looked over and saw the assassin. He stared, realizing how close he had come to being killed.

Andronicus turned slowly, and looked up at Thor. Slowly, he realized what Thor had just done. His expression of fear morphed to something like awe. Appreciation. It was an expression Thor had never seen on him before.

Andronicus rose and approached Thor slowly.

"My son," he said, reaching out and laying a hand on Thor's shoulder. "You have saved my life on this night."

Thor looked back at his father, filled with pride. In the past, the feel of Andronicus's touch had upset him; but now he welcomed it. It was his father's touch. The father he'd always longed to have.

"I did what any son would do," Thor replied.

Andronicus shook his head slowly, and looked down at Thor with admiration.

"I have vastly underestimated you," he said. "You are not only my greatest soldier. You are now also the son I never had. You are going to be by my side forever. Do you know that?"

Thor looked back into Andronicus' eyes, and he answered: "There is nothing I yearn for more, my father."

"Take a long look at me, Thornicus," he said. "Do you see who I am? My face, my height, my skin, my horns. I was not always this way. I was once like you. Like your father. Like my brothers. A MacGil, like all the others. But I changed. I transformed. I made a vow, and I accepted the powers of the darkest sorcery, and a ceremony was performed. I allowed the evil spirit to enter me. I allowed it to transform me. I allowed it to change my race, my appearance, and to give me more power than I'd ever dreamed. It is a sacred ceremony. Only a chosen few are given the privilege to transform, to attain such power."

Andronicus looked intensely into his eyes.

"You have proved yourself worthy here today. When these battles are over, you will transform, like me. You will be my height. My race. My skin. You will have horns, like mine. You will leave behind the pathetic human race. And you will become exactly as your father."

Thor's eyes glazed over, his mind clouded, as he was flooded with appreciation.

"I would like that father," he answered. "I would like that very much."

CHAPTER SEVENTEEN

Mycoples lay on the deck of the Empire ship, curled up in a ball beneath the Akron netting that clamped her down. Overwhelmed with sadness, she felt the rocking of the ocean beneath her, the gentle rise and fall of the boat, and she opened one eye just a bit. She saw Empire soldiers reveling, drinking, celebrating, clearly thrilled with themselves that they had subdued a dragon. She felt the aches all over her body from where they had poked and prodded and stabbed her.

She looked out, beyond them, and Mycoples saw the yellow waters of the Tartuvian, stretching as far as the eye could see. Mycoples closed her eyes again, wishing this would all just go away. She wished she could return to the land of her birth, to the land of the dragons, and be with her clan once again. Even more so, she wished that she could be at Thor's side. But she knew that Thor was far gone from her, lost in another place. He was not the Thorgrin she once knew.

Mycoples sensed that these soldiers would take her back to the Empire, put her on parade, make her a show-thing for the Empire soldiers. She sensed that she would be chained for the rest of her life, tortured, displayed like an artifact. As she thought of the misery of her life to come, it tortured her. She wished she could just die now, with pride, in one last great battle. She hadn't survived on this planet for thousands of years only for this, to be captured and held prisoner by humans. She had been warned never to get too close to a human, and she had made a mistake and allowed herself to be vulnerable. Her love for Thor had made her weak, had made her lower her defenses. And now she was paying the price.

Yet, despite it all, Mycoples still loved him—and she would do it all over again, just for him.

Mycoples closed her eyes, heavy from exhaustion, from the netting digging into her, from the wounds all over her body. And she wished only to be far from here.

*

Mycoples did not know how long she'd slept when she was awakened by a great whooshing noise. It sounded like an intense rain, and she felt her whole body become wet.

She looked up and saw that the ship was entering the Rain Wall. They were all suddenly immersed in a solid wall of rain, showering straight down on them. It was like going through a waterfall.

The Empire soldiers panicked, grabbing hold of the decks as the ship passed through. The noise became deafening. Mycoples welcomed it, the rain cooling her, steam rising off her scales from baking in the sun all these days. The pounding of the water momentarily took her mind off the troubles before her.

Slowly, they came out the other side.

Mycoples opened her eyes and saw that they had entered the red waters of the Sea of Blood. She realized the soldiers were taking the most direct route to the Empire, by circumventing the Isle of Mist.

Her heart fluttered as she felt a sudden flurry of hope. She had flown over the Isle of Mist with her clan many times. She knew it to be home to great warriors. And she also knew it to be home to something even more important: a rogue dragon. Ralibar.

Mycoples had met Ralibar once, centuries ago. He was a recluse, and he was unlike other dragons. He disliked his own kind; yet he disliked humans more. If they passed by, and Ralibar saw her in this predicament, perhaps he would come to her aid. Not because he liked her, but because he hated humans. Perhaps, he would even help free her.

Mycoples knew what she had to do: she had to somehow get this boat to sail to the Isle of Mist. She could not let them circumvent it. She had to get this boat directly onto the island. She had to get it to crash onto the island's rocks.

Mycoples closed her eyes and breathed deeply. She felt the sea air rushing through her scales, felt her body begin to tingle, as she summoned the last vestige of power she had. She called upon the Ancient Ones, who had guided her for thousands of years, to plead for one last favor. She did not ask for strength for herself. She did not even ask for the strength to battle.

Instead, she asked simply for the wind to answer her. The sky. The ocean. With her ancient, primordial dragon spirit, she summoned them all, called upon them to grant her this one favor. She asked for the wind to cry, the waves to rise, the skies to darken. She commanded them all, in the name of her ancestors, in the names of the ones who walked the planet before all others. Dragons had been here first. And dragons had the right to command nature.

Mycoples breathed, deeper and deeper, feeling herself grow warm; gradually, a wind stirred. The waves began to rise, to splash, and slowly, the boat tilted, then rose higher. The wind gained strength, and soon the sun hid itself, as the skies grew dark.

Soon, the boat was listing, as enormous waves rose up and fell over them; huge currents dragged them, the sky thundered, the wind was deafening, loud enough to drown out even the shouts of the Empire men who scurried all around her, running for their lives. Some fell overboard. They all tried to control the boat, but they could not: the boat was being blown off course.

Right for the Isle of Mist.

Mycoples opened her large, purple eyes and looked out with satisfaction: there it was, on the horizon, looming ever closer.

Over the howl of the wind, a lone sound arose, one that could be heard even far away, on the horizon, like an echo of a scream, filling the sky.

Mycoples smiled to herself. She knew that sound. She had been born to it. Had been raised with it all her life.

It was the cry of another dragon.

CHAPTER EIGHTEEN

Selese and Illepra charged across the endless hills and valleys of the Ring, as they had been all day and all night, heading for the Eastern Crossing for Reece. Selese rode with single-minded determination, and could think of nothing else. It had been a treacherous ride, taking the long way so as not to be seen, to avoid battlefields and random groups of soldiers and mercenaries. They had ridden through dark woods and over steep ridges to stay out of sight. More than once she'd feared they'd been spotted.

But it was all worth it. Selese would ride to the seven rings of hell to save Reece. And she felt he needed saving, sensed that he was in danger. He must be, on such a dangerous quest as he had embarked. Wherever the Destiny Sword was, she knew, death always followed.

She prayed she could get there in time, could help Reece from whatever dangers he might be in. Even if she couldn't, there was nowhere else she could be.

She had hardly stopped, her muscles weak from exhaustion, barely able to catch her breath; Illepra did not slow either. Illepra had become like a sister to her, and Selese was overwhelmed with gratitude for her being there. They both risked their lives to take this journey.

While they had done their best thus far to avoid open roads, they had reached a point, the final leg of their journey, where there was no way to avoid it. Now there was nothing but open landscape, a single, barren dusty road leading ever east. Trees gave way to rocks, and these to dirt, and then to nothing but a vast, barren desert. The Eastern Crossing would not be far now.

The only problem nagging at Selese was how exposed they were, on this open road, in the middle of nowhere. They were too visible, just the two of them riding alone. She felt very on-edge, the hairs on her arms standing up, as she felt prone to ambush from all sides. The Ring was torn apart, armies fighting armies, and even these armies divided amongst each other. It was a lawless, chaotic place to be right now, with no law and order, no one to stop bands of criminals. She knew they had to get to Reece fast.

They rounded a bend, and suddenly, Selese and Illepra stopped short. There, before them, blocking the road, was a huge, felled tree. She wondered how it could be there, in the middle of nowhere.

She heard a noise, and before she even spun around, she knew: they had been ambushed.

Behind them stood four soldiers, emerging from behind a boulder, all large and broad, unshaven, passing around a wine sack and drinking. She saw from their armor that they were Silesians. Her own kind. She knew she should feel relief.

Yet she did not: they were drunk, and they looked them over with lust in their eyes. They seemed far from the main army, and as she looked more carefully at their ragged armor, at the stripes torn from their uniforms, she realized: these were deserters. Spineless, rogue soldiers, betrayers to their own people. The worst of the worst.

"And where might you two fine ladies be off to now?" their leader asked, as the four of them made their way closer to them.

Selese's horse pranced, boxed in with nowhere to go. Her heart pounded in her throat, as she wondered how to handle this. She saw Illepra glancing at her nervously, and saw that Illepra was uncertain, too.

"We are Silesians, just as you," Illepra called out. "We serve the royal army. We are healers. So please let us pass. We have important business we must attend to."

"Do you?" he asked, stepping forward and grabbing the horse's reigns as another grabbed Selese's.

"We are from Silesia, as are you," Illepra repeated, her voice trembling.

"Ah, Silesia," he said, mocking. "And such eternal love we have for our people."

"You are deserters," Selese called out, her voice darker, more authoritative, less afraid, condemning the people before her. "The lowest of the low."

The others scowled, but the leader laughed and shook his head, surveying her.

"I'd say we are the smartest of the smart. We are the ones who survive, the ones who live for another day. We do not fight for some fake thing called chivalry, which we can neither see, nor touch, nor feel. Why should we fight someone else's war?"

"It is *your* Ring," Selese responded, undeterred. "It is *your* war."

"My war is to stay alive—or to fight for anyone who pays the highest price. But I've heard enough out of you."

He reached up and in one quick motion, grabbed Selese by her shirt and yanked her down.

Selese screamed as she went flying off her horse, landing hard on the ground, tumbling. She saw Illepra being yanked off her horse, too.

A soldier grabbed each of them, and yanked them to their feet, while the other two soldiers surrounded them. The leader leaned in, his face inches away from Selese's, so close she could see the pockmarks in his face and smell his bad breath. The rough stubble of his chin rubbed up against her cheek.

"This is our lucky day," he said. "We get two fine horses, and two fine girls to have our way with."

"Don't worry about your famed Silesia," another said, "you won't be seeing it for a long time."

He laughed, and the others joined in.

"You are making a great mistake," Selese said, her voice booming with confidence. "I'm on a journey to find Reece, the youngest son of King MacGil. The MacGils are a fierce and noble clan. If you harm us, and they find out what you've done, they will kill you all."

"And who says they will find out what we've done?" he asked back, grinning.

The leader pulled a dagger, and began to raise it towards Selese.

Selese knew she had to do something, and quick. Clearly, these men would not listen to reason. They were out for blood, and she had no weapons at her disposal.

Suddenly, Selese had an idea. It was risky, but it just might work.

Selese quietly slipped her hand to her side satchel and ran her finger inside until she found a small vial of liquid, feeling it by touch. She closed her fingers around it and held it in her palm.

She suddenly changed her expression, smiling at the leader, and said, in a sweet and sexy voice: "I will do whatever you say. In fact, I would like to. I find you quite attractive."

The leader leaned back and looked at her, surprised.

"All I ask is one thing," she added. "Just kiss me first. I want to feel your lips on mine. The lips of a real man. A real warrior."

The soldier looked back, confused and happily surprised. One of the others stepped up and patted him on the back.

"See, they listen to reason," he said. "They always do."

The leader grinned wide and brushed his shirt and ran a hand through his hair, tidying his appearance.

"That's more like it," he said.

"Selese, what are you doing?" Illepra asked, confused.

But Selese ignored her. She had a plan.

Selese pretended to yawn, raising her hand to her mouth, and placed the vial inside.

She leaned forward, grabbed the soldier's face, and kissed him, putting her lips on his.

As she did, she spat the vial into his open mouth. She then reached up and clamped his mouth shut.

He stared back at her, wide-eyed, and tried to resist.

But it was too late. She raised both hands and clamped his mouth firmly shut, forcing him to bite the vial in his mouth. She watched as his face turned bright red, the veins popping in his throat; he reached up and grabbed for his throat, gasping, and a second later he dropped to his knees, then collapsed.

Dead.

Of course he would be. That vial contained Blackox—the deadliest poison she carried.

The other three soldiers looked on, confused—and Selese did not give them a chance to figure it out.

Selese reached into her satchel and searched for Apoth, a yellow powder which was an effective salve when mixed with water—but deadly if it entered the eyes in powder form. She grabbed two handfuls.

"You little wench!" one screamed out, as he drew his dagger and charged.

She threw a handful into his eyes, and he shrieked. Selese then stepped forward and threw the other handful into the other two soldiers' eyes.

All of them shrieked, collapsing to their backs, writhing and foaming at the mouth.

Within seconds, they were all dead.

In the silence, Illepra looked at her, mouth open in shock, hardly able to conceive what had just happened.

Selese turned and looked back at her, hands shaking but feeling strong, determined. She didn't know if she could have done that if it was for herself; but thinking of Reece had made her stronger.

"Let's go," she said, mounting her horse. "It's past time we found Reece."

CHAPTER NINETEEN

Kendrick charged across the landscape, Erec, Bronson and Srog at his side and thousands of liberated troops riding behind them, all of them free, once again. They had been riding all night long, ever since they'd escaped the Empire camp, and had never slowed, putting as much distance between them as they could.

Now, finally, dawn was breaking. It had been a long and harrowing night, ever since Kendrick, Erec, Bronson and Srog had freed thousands of their men, had massacred their captors, and had ridden off while the bulk of the Empire soldiers were still asleep. They had not wanted to get embroiled in a full-scale encounter with the vast Empire forces in the middle of the night; rather, they moved quickly and stealthily, killing any troops who stood in their way. They reclaimed their horses and arms, and took off. They wanted to fight another day, on their own terms.

Here, on the McCloud side of the kingdom, Bronson knew the terrain, and he led them expertly. Kendrick knew they were lucky to have him, as he was proving an invaluable guide to help hide them from the Empire. Kendrick and Erec had asked Bronson to lead them to a terrain where they could be well-hidden from the Empire, yet also from which they could attack a smaller division. They would have to switch tactics, and it was time for a new strategy now: instead of facing off with the entire Empire army, they would have to find a smaller division—just a few thousand men, to match their own few thousand—and wage smaller battles, before retreating again. Being so outnumbered, the only way to success would be to wage a prolonged, guerilla war. They could stick to the mountains, stay well hidden in the Highlands, and be a lethal fighting force, attacking strategically, like a snake, then retreating. They may not have the same numbers and strength, but they had the willpower to outwait the Empire.

They rode and rode, and followed Bronson's lead as he turned off a steep trail, leading them right up one side of the Highlands. They had been following an old trail of the Empire, taking them past waves of destruction, from one McCloud town to the next. Finally, the trail stopped here, at the top of a particular peak.

They all slowed their horses and came to a stop.

"Highlandia," Bronson called out, pointing.

From this vantage point, at a distant peak, Kendrick saw, across the mountain range, Highlandia, the small McCloud city, perched high up, on the very edge of the Highlands, straddling the Eastern and Western kingdoms of the Ring. Even in the dawn, he could see that Andronicus's forces occupied it. He saw their fires still smoldering, noted the heads of prisoners on pikes throughout the city, and he could tell that they had recently massacred the McClouds here.

There appeared to be several thousand men encamped about the city, and it was hard to tell how many more lay within. He could not tell if this was the bulk of the Empire army, or just a lone division.

"This might be a prime city for us to attack," Kendrick said.

"Highlandia is a small city, but a strategic point at the peak of the Highlands," Bronson said. "It makes sense that Andronicus would take it. From here, is a straight ride down to the Western kingdom, the roads branching in all directions. It would be his first stop to crush the McCloud resistance and launch a final attack on the Western Kingdom and dominate the Ring."

"But is Andronicus himself inside?" Srog asked. "And how many men with him?"

They all surveyed it. It was hard to tell.

"It could be risky," Bronson said. "Perhaps it would be better to hide out here in the mountains, and wait for a smaller group to attack, or a smaller city."

Kendrick shook his head.

"No more waiting," he said. "Any day could be our last. Never again will I subject myself to imprisonment by anyone. If we are to die, we will die on our feet. We attack now!"

"I am with you!" Erec said, drawing his sword.

"And I!" Bronson said.

"So be it!" Srog said.

They all kicked their horses and charged along the edge of the Highlands, weaving in and out of the steep mountain trails, racing towards Highlandia. In the breaking dawn, with most Empire troops still sleeping, perhaps they would have the advantage of surprise, Kendrick thought. Perhaps they could take this city, and make it a stronghold of their own. Maybe, if they could wait long enough, Gwendolyn would return, with Argon. And maybe, just maybe, the tide could turn in their favor.

Even if not, this was what they were born to do: to attack against the odds, to never cower from the enemy, to fight for the right cause, even when the odds seemed impossible. Kendrick had been given a great privilege in his life: he had been given a grant of arms. They all had. And he intended to use it, as long as he was still alive.

An Empire horn sounded, then another, then another, all along the parapets of the small castle of Highlandia. Suddenly, the tall iron, portcullis opened, and hundreds of Empire soldiers appeared, charging right for them. They were not sleeping: they had been ready, and waiting.

Nonetheless, Kendrick let out a great battle cry of his own and charged harder, prepared to fight, to kill anyone who dared stand in his way.

But as he got closer, as the Empire soldiers came into view, he saw a face charge through the gate, a face that made his blood run cold. It was the only face that could make him lower his sword, make his mouth drop open in shock, and make him nearly fall off his horse.

There, facing him, riding out to meet him, sword raised high, was a man he loved like a brother.

There was Thorgrin.

CHAPTER TWENTY

Thornicus rode beside his father, Rafi and McCloud behind them, as they lead thousands of Empire soldiers out the gates of Highlandia, prepared to crush the enemy. Thor looked out and saw riding towards them thousands of soldiers, dressed in an armor and waving a banner that he dimly recognized. As they neared, a part of him recognized it as the armor he once knew, the armor of the Western Kingdom of the ring, of the Silver, of the MacGils. Thor was momentarily confused; he wondered why he was attacking these people he had once fought with side-by-side.

But his mind just as quickly became clouded, and another part of him, a stronger part, reminded him that he was riding to crush the enemies of his father, riding to kill those who would kill his father first. Thornicus felt infused with a new energy, determined to kill them all, to prevent anyone from harming Andronicus, or the Empire.

He charged towards the MacGil soldiers, still perhaps a half mile away, drawing his sword, leading the army, getting ready to attack with all he had.

But suddenly, a chorus of horns sounded out behind him, and Andronicus and the others turned and checked back over their shoulders. Thor did, too. It was a sound of distress, and as Thor turned, he was confused by what he saw: hundreds of Empire soldiers were turning around, and charging in the reverse direction. Beyond them, in the distance, thousands of Empire soldiers, of a different division, charged up the ridge for Highlandia, torches in hand, and began to set fire to the city.

"What's happening, my master?" McCloud called out to Andronicus, as confused as the rest of them.

Andronicus looked confused himself; but then, as he watched the horizon, his eyes narrowed in recognition.

"Romulus," he said knowingly. "My general has come to betray me."

Thousands of Empire troops attacked them from the rear, flooding the city. Now they were sandwiched between two armies, Romulus's men behind them and the MacGil soldiers before them.

Andronicus screamed out in frustration, debating, then finally turned his horse around.

"We must save Highlandia!" Andronicus shouted. "Abandon the MacGils! Attack Romulus!"

Andronicus kicked his horse, turning around sharply, and Thornicus and the others followed, preparing to engage the Empire soldiers in a civil war.

As he turned around, Thornicus glanced back over his shoulder, and in the distance, he saw the MacGils continue to charge, for Highlandia. But that was no longer Thor's concern; he had to do his father's bidding. They could fight the MacGils another day.

Thor rode with his father, and he held his sword high. He and Andronicus rode side-by-side, and it felt good to ride with him. They were in unison, together in battle, prepared to face the world together, as father and son should.

The two of them charged down the slope, aiming for Romulus' men, and they all met halfway, in a great clash of arms. Thousands of warriors rushed headlong into each other; leading the fray, the first into battle, was Andronicus. He raised his great battle ax, swung it in the air, and met Romulus as he charged for his former boss. Romulus swung his axe, too, and the two of them locked, like rams, each as powerful as the other, each wanting to kill the other with all his heart.

Thor aimed for Romulus' commander, and the commander raised his shield, but it did little good: Thor's blow was so strong, it sliced the shield in half. The commander raised his sword to slash back, but Thor was too fast. He kept charging, and with another blow, slashed the man across the stomach, making him slump forward, face first into the dirt.

The sound of clashing metal filled Thor's ears as all around them, thousands of soldiers fought hand to hand. None fought so deftly as Thor. He slashed and parried and ducked and weaved in every direction, taking down dozens of men before they could move quickly enough to react to him. He cut through the men like a single man army, felling soldiers left and right, and pushing the stalemate in favor of Andronicus.

Due to Thor's efforts, the tide began to turn between the two equally matched divisions. Romulus initially had the advantage of surprise and momentum, since no Empire men had expected to be fighting each other on this day. But Thor tipped the odds, single-handedly pushing back more and more of Romulus' men as they poured in to try to take Highlandia.

Romulus and Andronicus went blow for blow, cracking their great battle axes into each other with a shrill clang of metal, like two old rams battling for power. Andronicus was much taller than Romulus, but Romulus was so wide, and he had strength unlike any Thor had ever seen. They were a spectacle to watch, like two mountains, neither seeming able to give into the other.

A wounded soldier fell onto the back on Andronicus' horse, and Andronicus' horse pranced, off-balance; the loss of balance was just enough to give Romulus a slight advantage. Andronicus' axe lowered momentarily, just enough for Romulus to land a blow, slicing him hard on the shoulder, and knocking Andronicus off his horse.

Romulus wasted no time: he dismounted, raised his axe high with both hands, and preparing to bring it down on Andronicus' exposed head.

Thor's heart fell; he dove off his horse, face-first, and tackled Romulus down to the ground, right before Romulus could land the deadly blow. They stumbled back several feet, and the two fell and wrestled in the mud, rolling again and again, soldiers dying all around them.

Finally, Romulus gained the upper hand, rolling and throwing Thor off him. He pulled a dagger from his waist, and aimed it for Thor's throat; it all happened too quickly for Thor to react.

Andronicus appeared and knocked the blade from Romulus' hand before it could hurt Thor, saving his life.

Andronicus then swung for Romulus' head with his axe; but Romulus rolled out of the way, and the axe lodged instead in the mud.

A horn sounded, and the sky darkened with arrows. Romulus' men fell left and right, screaming out in pain, scores of them felled by arrows as Andronicus' reinforcements arrived. The tide of the battle had turned.

Romulus' men began to retreat. Romulus, seeing what was happening, no longer challenged Andronicus; instead, he ducked throughout the crowd, found his horse, kicked hard, and turn and fled with his remaining men.

Andronicus saw Thor on the ground, realized he had been saved by him once again, and his heart welled with gratitude. He reached a hand down to pull up his son.

Thornicus took his father's hand, realizing his father had saved his life, too. They stood there, clasping hands, father and son, each sacrificing their lives for the other. Andronicus looked down at Thor with respect, and Thor returned it. Finally, Thor had found the father he had always craved in life.

CHAPTER TWENTY ONE

Romulus charged with his fleeing men, downhill, away from Highlandia, infuriated. He was shocked at his defeat. He had never lost a battle before, and he could not reconcile it. He had overreached. He should have stuck to his original plan to find a MacGil, cross the Canyon, and attack with his full army; instead, he went for the quick and hasty kill. He had become too emboldened, too confident. He had made the mistake of an amateur commander, and he hated himself for it.

Romulus had experienced multiple failures. His initial plot had been to send an assassin to kill Andronicus in the night, and somehow that had failed. His second plot had been to rally his men at dawn, to use his newfound momentum to come upon Andronicus unaware, and to take a quick stab at murdering him. He knew he'd be outnumbered, but he thought, if only he could kill him quickly, then it wouldn't matter; all the remaining Empire men would of course rally under his command at once.

In retrospect, it was a hasty and rash decision, and he should have waited. He should have lowered the Shield first, and then attacked in force. There were no shortcuts to victory.

Romulus kept replaying in his mind how close he had come, and that was what upset him most. He'd almost had Andronicus and surely would have killed him if it had not been for Thornicus. He had not expected Thornicus to be there, by Andronicus' side, and had not expected such a lethal adversary. Andronicus would be dead right now if it weren't for him. When all this settled down, Romulus vowed to kill Thor himself. The idea of that cheered him up: he would kill father and son together. At least he had escaped, unlike many of his men.

Now he rode towards his second objective. On the ride across the Ring Romulus had slaughtered and tortured many soldiers along the way, for the fun of it. He had also interrogated them, and had learned of the MacGil who had been captured by Andronicus: Luanda. MacGil's firstborn daughter. She would do perfectly.

Romulus rode now to where the soldiers had told him she would be, on the outskirts of the camp. He was ready to execute his backup plan. He rode hard, and finally reached it; he went to the stocks and found the lone girl bound to a post, her hair shaved off. That was her: Luanda, half dressed, bruised and beaten, a bloody mess. She was tied to the post, barely conscious, and Romulus did not even slow his horse as he galloped right towards her.

He raised his great axe high and chopped off her ropes, then with his other hand he reached down and grabbed her roughly by the shirt, and in one motion hoisted her onto the front of his horse.

Luanda, panic stricken, screamed, struggling to get away.

But Romulus did not give her the chance. He reached over with his huge arm and wrapped it entirely around her body, firmly, squeezing her tightly against him. The feel of her in his arms felt good. If he did not need her to bring across the bridge, he might have his way with her now, then kill her on the spot. But he needed her to lower the Shield, and there was little time to waste.

Romulus kicked his horse and rode twice as fast, forking away from his men, taking the lone road that head to the Canyon. When he was done with her, he could always kill her then, just for fun.

Romulus rode with a smile, and the more Luanda screamed, fighting and protesting, the more he smiled. He had his prize. Soon they would be at the bridge, over the crossing.

Finally, the shield would be lowered. His army would invade. And the Ring would be his for all time.

CHAPTER TWENTY TWO

Reece lay on the ground at the base of the Canyon, ribs aching, and looked up as the razor-sharp teeth of the beast, emerging from its jaw and plunged down to kill him. He knew that in moments, those teeth would sink into his chest and tear out his heart. He braced himself for the agony to come.

There came an awful shriek, and at first Reece was sure it was his own.

Then he opened his eyes and realized it was the shriek of the beast, an awful scream, piercing the air and rising up to the heavens. The beast leaned back its head and roared and roared, flailing its arms wildly. Then suddenly, it became very still, keeled over, and lay perfectly still.

Dead.

The world, once again, was still.

Reece sat up, eyes wide with wonder, trying to comprehend what had just happened. How had this beast, which had injured them all, suddenly died?

Reece noticed a spear sticking through the right foot of the beast, embedded in the ground. There, standing over the beast, wielding the spear with a self-satisfied grin, stood a stranger. He was tall and thin, with a short beard, wearing rags, with long, shaggy hair. He was skinny, perhaps in his late forties, and he smiled back infectiously.

"You always kill a Lombok through its foot," he explained, as if it were the most obvious thing, extracting his spear out of the ground. "That's where its heart is. Didn't you ever learn that?"

The stranger stepped forward, held out a palm, and Reece grabbed it and let him pull him to his feet. The man, though skinny, was surprisingly strong.

Reece looked back, still stunned, hardly knowing how to react. This man had just saved his life.

"I...um..." he stammered. "I...don't know how to thank you."

"Thank me?" the man repeated. He leaned back and laughed, then clasped a warm hand on Reece's shoulder, friendly, turning and walking with him. "There's nothing to thank me for, good friend. I hate Lomboks. They take my traps every time and leave me hungry every other night. No, thank me not at all. You did me a favor. You got it out in the open, and made it an easy kill."

The man surveyed Reece's group, and shook his head.

"Such a shame. All fine warriors. You were just aiming for the wrong spot."

"Who are you?" O'Connor asked, coming over. "Where do you hail from? What are you doing down here?"

The man laughed heartily.

"I am Centra. Pleased to meet you all, but I can't answer so many questions at once. I came down here many years ago—just curious, I guess. I couldn't stand living under the thumb of the McClouds. I used a series of ropes to scale down the Canyon wall, and I never came back up. Out of choice. At first I was just exploring, but I grew to like it down here, all to myself. Exotic. Do you know what I mean? I'm a loner, so I don't mind not having the company. But I must say, you're the first human faces I've seen since, and it feels good to see my people. To strength!"

Centra pulled a wine sack from his waist and leaned back and drank. He then held it up and motioned for Reece's mouth.

Reece didn't know what to say, and he didn't want to offend him, so he tentatively opened his mouth, and let Centra squirt the liquid in. It landed on the back of Reece's throat, and burned, and Reece coughed.

Centra laughed aloud.

"What is it?" Reece asked, gasping, as Centra went around and squirted it in each person's mouth.

"Atibar," he answered. "It flows in a stream not far from here. Burns, does it? But how does it make you feel?"

Reece felt a tingling run up and down his body, and soon he felt lightheaded, relaxed. He definitely felt less on-edge; he didn't feel the pains and bumps and bruises all over his body as acutely as he had.

As the others finished their round, Centra reached out and offered more to Reece; but this time Reece held up a hand and stopped him.

"Have some more my friend," Centra said. "It wears off quickly."

Reece shook his head.

"Thank you, but I need my head clear."

"You saved our lives," Elden said, stepping forward in all seriousness. "And that is something we take very seriously. We owe you a great debt. Name your price. Men of the Legion always honor what they owe."

Centra shook his head.

"You owe me nothing. But if it makes you happy, I'll tell you what: help me find a good meal for the night. That damn Lombok stole it. I want to get something before nightfall."

"We will help you any way we can," Reece said.

Centra surveyed the group.

"And why are you all down here, if I may ask?"

"We have come on urgent business," Reece replied. "Have you seen the Sword?"

"The Sword?" Centra asked, eyebrows raised high. "What sword? It seems to me you are carrying a sword."

Reece shook his head.

"No, *the* Sword. The Destiny Sword. It was embedded in a boulder. It plummeted over the edge."

Centra's eyes opened wide.

"The actual Destiny Sword?" he said, awe in his voice. "It is not down here, is it?"

Reece nodded.

"But how can it be? It is the sword of legend. What on earth would it be doing down here? In any case, I have seen no boulders, nor any swords. Are you sure—wait a minute," he said, stopping himself. "Wait a minute," he said, rubbing his chin, "you don't mean the explosion, do you?"

Reece and the others looked at each other, puzzled.

"Explosion?" O'Connor asked.

"Earlier, something fell down from high above," Centra said, "so loud, it shook the whole place. I didn't see it, but I felt it. Who didn't? It left a huge crater."

Reece's heart raced faster.

"Crater?" Reece asked. "That would make sense. The boulder *would* make a crater, from that high up." He stepped closer to Centra and asked in all seriousness: "Can you lead us there?"

Centra shrugged.

"I don't see why not. The best game lies in that direction anyway. Follow me. But be quick about it: you don't want to be walking about at nightfall. Not when the night mist swirls."

Centra turned and took off quickly, and Reece and the others fell in behind him, O'Connor and Elden helping to carry Krog as he limped heavily. All of them were slow to regroup from their battle, rubbing their wounds, gathering their weapons, walking stiffly, none of them moving as fast or as limber as they were before. That battle with the Lombok had taken its toll; Reece realized again how lucky they were to make it out alive.

They marched in the mud, in and out of the brightly-colored woods, and they followed Centra as he weaved a dizzying path, following some invisible trail that only he must have known. Reece could see no discernible sign of a path, but clearly Centra knew where he was going. The swirling mists blew in and out, and Reece wondered how on earth Centra was able to navigate this place. It all looked the same to him, and if it weren't for Centra, he realized he would be inextricably lost.

It was getting darker as they went, and Reece was getting concerned. The sound of animals never stopped, and he could not help but wonder which creatures came out here at night? If the Lombok existed, what other creatures might there be?

They marched and marched, and just as Reece was about to ask Centra how much farther, suddenly they stumbled upon a gap in the trees. All the trees here had been flattened, their branches broken, the trees pushed back at unnatural angles. He walked more quickly, catching up to Centra, and Centra suddenly reached up and put a rough palm on Reece's chest, stopping him from taking another step forward.

Reece stopped short and realized he was lucky Centra had stopped him. As the mist rose, right beneath them, at the edge of his feet, there was revealed a huge crater, at least twenty feet in diameter and sinking a good twenty yards down into the earth. It looked as if a meteor had fallen from the sky and destroyed an entire section of the forest.

Reece's heart pounded as he knew immediately that this must be the crater left by the plummeting of the boulder.

Reece searched excitedly for the Sword. All the others came up beside them, peering down over the edge, shocked.

But as the mist cleared, Reece was shocked and disappointed to see the crater was empty.

"How can it be?" O'Connor asked, beside him.

"It's not possible," Elden said.

"The boulder is not there," Indra said.

"Perhaps this is a different crater," Serna said.

Reece turned to Centra.

"Are you sure this is the spot?" Reece asked.

Centra nodded vigorously.

"This is it," he said. "I am certain. I was not far when it happened, and I came to look for myself. I noticed a large stone, with a piece of metal in it, now that you mention it. I didn't think much of it."

"Then where is it?" Elden asked, skeptical.

"I am not lying," Centra said indignantly.

Reece examined the floor of the crater carefully, and as the mist cleared, he noticed tracks leading up one side of it. It looked as if the boulder had been dragged up one side of the crater.

Reece walked over to it quickly, as did the others, and as got close, he realized it was definitely the trail of the boulder, wide and deep, being slid away. All around, were dozens of footprints. They were strange prints, too small to be quite human.

Centra stood over them, kneeled down in the mud, and he reached down and fingered the prints knowingly.

"Faws," he said.

"What is that?" Reece asked.

"These are their tracks. They are a hostile tribe. Scavengers. It makes sense. They live on the far side of the Canyon. They *would* come and salvage something like this. They salvage anything they can find."

"What do you mean?" Indra pressed. "They took the boulder? How could they have the strength?"

Centra sighed.

"They move as one. There are thousands of them. Together, they can do anything, like worker ants. They live that way," he said, pointing. "Well, that's that. Sorry about your Sword. But if the Faws have it, you can't get it back."

"Why do you say that?" Reece asked.

"They are a vicious and hostile tribe," Centra said. "Savage warriors. Part human, part something else. Everyone down here knows to stay clear of them. They're like a mill of ants. Come near them, and they have a system of alerting each other. They would kill you before you got close. No one will survive."

Reece grasped the hilt of his sword, and stepped forward.

"Just the kind of odds I like."

CHAPTER TWENTY THREE

Gwendolyn stood before the ice monster, frozen in terror. Beside her, the others stood frozen, too, looking up at the beast in wonder. Gwen was flooded with fear, and a part of her wanted to turn and run, or at least raise her hands up and brace herself from an attack.

But another part of her forced her to be strong, to stand her ground and fight. Some small part of her knew she had the strength, and that she needed to be strong, not just for herself, but for the others. She couldn't run from her fears; she might die facing them, but then, at least, she would die with honor. After all, she was a King's daughter, and the blood of royalty ran in her.

The monster swooped its arm around towards her, its five jaws at the end of its five fingers snapping open and shut as it neared. Gwen, with shaking hands, drew her sword, and stepped forward and swung at it.

The sword missed, the monster much quicker than she'd anticipated. Where his hand had been a second before, there was now nothing but air.

The monster's jaws snapped open and shut, an awful noise of chattering teeth, and it lunged forward with a high-pitched squeaking noise, emanating from each of its ten jaws. They lunged right for Gwendolyn.

Gwendolyn screamed out in pain as one of its small jaws bit her arm, clamping down, drawing blood. She tried to pull away, but there was no use: the monster had clamped down tight, and she could feel its teeth sinking into her skin.

Gwen heard a snarl, and Krohn lunged forward and leapt onto the beast, biting the offending finger. Krohn clamped his jaws down on the monster's hand, refusing to let go, shaking his head left and right, snarling, until finally, the monster loosened its grip.

Gwen quickly stepped back, the pain shooting through her arm, and reached up and clasped her arm. Her hand was stained with blood, and she tore off a strip of cloth from the end of her shirt and tied it with a shaking hand around the wound, stopping the blood.

The monster turned to Krohn, in a rage. Another one of its jaws wheeled around, and with a sudden strike, it bit Krohn in the leg.

Krohn yelped, yet he would still not loosen his bite on the monster's hand, chomping down on the monster's fingers with all his might, until finally he snapped one of its jaws off. The monster shrieked, and Krohn fell to the ground, taking one of the monster's fingers with it.

The monster, in a rage, leaned back and swung its arm around, preparing to sink several more of its mouths into Krohn's back.

Steffen stepped forward, took aim, and fired two arrows in quick succession at the beast. Each arrow lodged itself in the monster's small jaw, an incredible feet from that far away, and at such a fast-moving target. It caused the monster to turn away from Krohn, sparing him.

It turned instead and faced Steffen, irate, and roared.

The monster charged for Steffen, its arms and jaws flailing at the end of its fingers, the sound of cracking ice filling the air as it charged for Steffen. Steffen was out of arrows, and as he fumbled with his bow, Aberthol lunged forward, his staff before him, boldly raised it with both hands, and jabbed it into the monster's chest.

Despite the noble effort, the staff blow was useless against such a powerful beast; the monster merely looked down at Aberthol as if he were an annoying insect, and reached back and backhanded him. The sound of ice smacking skin cut through the air, and Aberthol, with a groan, went flying, landing hard on his back on the ice and sliding back several feet before he came to a stop, moaning in pain.

The monster focused again on Steffen. As Steffen backed up, the monster jumped forward, reached down, scooped Steffen up with one hand, raised him high overhead, a good twenty feet in the air, and examined him as if he were a meal. The monster turned Steffen upside down, then reached over with its other hand, and aimed its snapping jaws for Steffen's face.

Gwen realized with horror that it was about to eat Steffen alive.

As Steffen had been hoisted in the air, he dropped his bow and arrows, and Gwen, thinking quick, ran over and snatched them off the ground. With shaking hands, she took aim.

Gwen fired several arrows, embedding them in the monster's side, and, finally, in one of its jaws.

It turned and glared at her, shrieking with rage, and dropped Steffen to the ground. Steffen hurled end-over-end through the air, and hit the ice with a cracking noise. Gwen hoped he had not broken all his bones.

The monster descended for Gwen once again, this time with both hands outreached, all its jaws snapping; Gwen, out of arrows and with nowhere to run, knew that it was about to kill her. Still, she did not regret it, as she had at least saved Steffen's life.

"BY THE LAWS OF THE SEVEN CIRCLES OF NATURE, I COMMAND YOU TO HALT!" boomed a fierce voice.

Gwendolyn turned to see Alistair step forward, hold out a palm and aim it at the creature. An orange ball of light shot from it and went to the creature, hitting it in the chest.

But the creature turned to Alistair, unafraid, and swatted away the light ball as it approached. The ball went flying harmlessly over his shoulder.

Alistair stood there, shocked. Clearly, she had not been expecting that.

The monster instead turned and rushed for Alistair. It kicked her, its huge claws impacting her chest and sending her flying backwards, skidding across the ice.

Not satisfied, the monster bore down on her, preparing to finish her off.

Gwen took stock of the battlefield, and it did not look good: Alistair was on her back, and Steffen, Aberthol and Krohn lay there moaning, all injured by the monster. Gwen herself lay there, smarting from the blow, and she wondered how they could ever defeat this thing. Their weapons were too flimsy against such a creature, and even Alistair's druid magic had not worked.

Gwen turned and scanned her surroundings desperately, trying to use her wit, desperate to find something, anything that could be used, *some* way out of here. As she looked, she spotted something, and she had an idea.

There, at the top of one of the ice mounds, sat a large, round ice boulder. It was immense, and perched precariously, a good fifty feet high. It looked like one good shove could knock it from its perch— and the monster stood directly at the base of the ice mound beneath it. If Gwen could somehow dislodge the boulder, she could crush the beast below.

Gwendolyn burst into action. She ran and picked up Steffen's bow, placed an arrow, and took aim, firing at the ice ledge beneath the boulder. Her aim was perfect: she managed to lodge the arrow precisely beneath the boulder, cracking the ice—and the boulder swayed just a tiny bit.

But it just did not roll.

There were four arrows left, and with the monster bearing down on Alistair, there was little time to lose. Gwen fired again and again, and with her incredible aim, all four shots hit, as she'd hoped, in the exact same spot. Each time, the boulder rolled a little bit more.

It still sat on the precipice, tantalizingly about to go over the edge; but then it rolled backwards, and stopped. It didn't work. Gwendolyn was out of arrows. She had failed.

Alistair regained her feet, and she looked over and noticed what Gwendolyn was attempting to do. As the monster rushed for her, feet away, Alistair turned, raised both palms high above her head, and this time, she aimed for the ice boulder.

A yellow light shot from her palms, aimed up high at the ice mound, and the light flew across the battlefield. As she held the yellow light on the ice, beneath the boulder, it began to melt. Then crack.

Soon, the boulder began to move.

The monster was now just feet away, and Gwen feared that if the boulder did not roll quickly enough, Alistair would be killed before her eyes.

But Alistair, fearless, did not budge and did not back away in the face of the monstrous charge. She merely continued to concentrate, sending light onto the ice.

"ALISTAIR!" Gwen shrieked, running towards her.

The monster reached Alistair, grabbed her, and hoisted her high over its head with an awful shriek. Gwen could see that it was about to kill her.

There came a great whooshing noise, then the sound of ice cracking, and Gwen looked over to see the boulder released from its perch and rolling down the ice mound with a fury. Just as the monster pulled Alistair towards its open jaws to eat her, the boulder suddenly smashed into the monster's back.

The monster was completely crushed. It let out an awful death shriek as it was completely flattened beneath the boulder. Alistair went flying through the air as the monster let go, and she landed far away, luckily, in a snow bank.

Soon, all was still. A heavy silence hung in the air.

Gwendolyn, in shock, hurried over to Alistair, rushing to her side, checking to see if she was okay. Alistair lay there, dazed, but she opened her eyes and took Gwendolyn's hand and allowed her to pull her to her feet.

"Are you okay?" Gwen asked. She felt as if her own sister has been injured, and realized how much she cared for Alistair.

Alistair nodded back, looking shaken but unhurt.

Gwen broke into a smile, relieved.

They turned and hurried over to Steffen and Aberthol, helping each to their feet; they were bruised and beaten, but okay. Gwen then hurried over to Krohn, who whined on his side. She helped him up, and he licked her face. He was a bit unsteady, but okay, too.

The five of them stood there, dazed and confused, looking out at their surroundings, at these ice mounds, with a whole new respect and wonder. As Gwendolyn scanned the horizon, she was beginning to realize the true danger of this place. For the first time, she was beginning to wonder if they would ever find Argon.

Had it been madness to come here after all?

*

Gwen hiked and hiked, her knees weak, her body weary, pains radiating in her stomach. They hiked towards the large, scarlet ball of the setting sun, and they had been hiking all day. It felt like months. There was no end in sight: just the endless monotony of this landscape. She wondered how much longer they could keep this up, before they all just collapsed onto the ice.

They marched and marched through the fantastical valley of the mounds, all of them frozen to the bone. Luckily, since their last encounter, they had not encountered any other monsters. They had passed various small animals, creatures that Gwen had never seen before, most some shade of white, with small, glowing blue eyes—but these all scurried out of way as they went. Everywhere they went, Gwendolyn searched for any possible sign of Argon, but he was nowhere in sight.

As the last glimmer of sun began to disappear, Gwendolyn began to notice a slight change in the appearance of the landscape. This valley of ice mounds culminated in one huge mound, stretching as far as the eye could see, blocking their path. There was no way forward without climbing it.

They all stopped, hands on their hips, breathing hard, and looked up at the mound, maybe fifty feet high. They were exhausted. They all were hopeless, as if no longer believing they would ever find Argon—much less survive.

"What do you think?" Gwen asked, turning to the others.

"We have no choice," Alistair said. "Either we climb it, or we turn back."

Gwen knew she was right. But her legs, shaking, were so exhausted. They all stood there and stared up at the mound.

Finally, Alistair took the first step, and Gwen and the others, weary beyond exhaustion, followed.

Gwen, breathing hard, took one step after the other. It was a steep incline, and they all slipped as they went, Gwendolyn leaning forward with her palms on the ice, sliding, trying to steady herself.

Slowly, foot by foot, they fought their way to the top. As they made it, they all collapsed on their hands and knees.

"I can't go on," Aberthol gasped.

As Gwen lay there, gasping, she mustered just enough energy to lift her head, to look out on the other side of the mound. Her eyes opened wide in shock.

Gwen reached over and prodded the others, shoving them, forcing them to look, too.

"Look!" she insisted.

The others slowly raised their heads and saw what she did. The sight took her breath away. There, before them, was another sweeping valley. But this one was different than the others; this one was filled with what looked like ice capsules. As far as the eye could see, there were thousands and thousands of them, each about eight feet tall, a few feet wide, and each containing something.

As Gwen narrowed her eyes, she realized that each contained a body. Inside each was one person, frozen solid. Thousands of people, spread out every ten feet or so, like a huge graveyard, protruding vertically from the ice.

"The Valley of Trapped Souls," Aberthol said, in awe.

The others all stared, and no one needed to utter a word to know what was on everyone's mind. There, below, were people. Trapped. Gwen knew that somewhere there, down below, trapped amidst these people, was the person she had come to seek.

She breathed deep, and said what was on everyone's minds:

"Argon."

CHAPTER TWENTY FOUR

Andronicus stood beside Thornicus, just the two of them alone on the hillside against the setting sun, surveying the damage from their battle against Romulus. Andronicus stood beside his son, and could not be more proud. For the first time in his life, he felt an emotion other than anger, other than a desire for vengeance. For the first time, he was not burning with a desire to destroy and kill and torture everything in his path. Instead, he was experiencing an emotion he did not quite understand. As he thought of all that Thor had done, as he thought of how Thor had saved his life, twice, he felt more than pride. He felt concern for the boy. He felt something that might even be love.

The emotion terrified him, and Andronicus immediately quashed it, pushed it down deep in his consciousness, unable to deal with it. It was an emotion he was unused to, and it was too powerful, too overwhelming.

Instead, he merely looked down at Thor with a much safer emotion, one he could understand: pride in victory. Thor had turned out to be a far greater asset than he could have ever imagined.

He draped his long fingernails over Thor's shoulder.

"You have saved my life on the battlefield today," Andronicus said.

Thornicus stood beside him, eyes glazed, gazing out at the carnage. Andronicus wondered if Thor would continue to serve him if Rafi took away the spell. Deep down, he hoped that he would, hoped that Thor had come to love him, too, in his own right, as any son would a father. He secretly hoped that as Rafi lifted the spell, after enough time went by, Thor might become loyal to Andronicus in his own right, might come to see him as the true father that he was.

Andronicus surveyed the damage, saw all of his men dead, saw all of the rebellious Empire men dead, and he knew that he owed Thorgrin his life. That was something he had never anticipated.

All around them their came screams, as Andronicus' men tortured any surviving Empire soldiers who had betrayed him. Andronicus breathed deeply, satisfied at the sound. It was time to make all the traitors pay, and to send a message to anyone else who dared defy him. Romulus was on the run, and Andronicus would stop at nothing to find him and put an end to him for good.

First, though, Andronicus had more pressing matters. He turned and looked up and surveyed, in the distance, Highlandia, destroyed by the rebels. He stood there, hands on his hips, surveying it with chagrin. Highlandia had been his; if it hadn't been for Romulus attacking him from the rear, if he hadn't had to turn around to pursue him, they would not have had to abandon the city. Andronicus grimaced as he realized the damage Kendrick, Erec and the others had done, taking out several thousand of his men while the main army was distracted. They had since fled, who knew where, back into the safety of the mountains. Andronicus surveyed the mountains, but it was getting dark and it would be too hard to find them now. In the morning, though, they would prod them out, like weasels, and kill them all. With Thornicus at his side, now anything was possible.

"In the morning, we will find and kill whomever remains of your former friends," Andronicus stated.

"I am at your service, my father," Thor said.

Andronicus was mollified at the words. He turned and looked over at Thorgrin.

"I owe you a great debt. No one has saved my life before. Tell me what I can give you in return. Name it. Anything in the Empire is yours."

Thor gazed out for a long time, as if lost in another world, and Andronicus wondered if he would ever reply.

Then, finally, Thorgrin spoke softly:

"My mother's ring," he said.

Andronicus looked down at him in surprise.

"It was stolen from me by one of your men," Thor said. "I want it back."

Andronicus nodded.

"You shall have it."

Andronicus snapped his fingers, one of his generals came running, and Andronicus whispered in his ear, and shoved him off. The general turned and sprinted, rushing to execute his command.

"It will be found quickly, my son," Andronicus said. "Or else the general himself will be dead by morning."

Thor nodded, pleased.

"I will also torture and execute personally the man who stole it from you," Andronicus said.

"I do not need anyone tortured or executed," Thor said. "I just want it back."

"They will be tortured and executed whether you like it or not," Andronicus said back firmly. "That is my way. Soon, it will be your way, too."

Andronicus sighed.

"In the morning, we will battle and crush the remainder of your former people, and then our kingdom will be complete. Side by side, together, we will rule it forever."

Thorgrin turned and stared back at his father, and Andronicus sensed complete agreement in him.

"There is nothing I would cherish more, my father."

*

Thornicus lay on the ground in the black of night, close to Andronicus and the rest of the Empire soldiers, beside the crackling bonfire, lying on the cold dirt and rocks. He dreamt troubled dreams.

Thor found himself standing in an open field, looking out, prepared for battle. Before him were thousands of men on horseback, and as he looked closer, he noticed they all sat oddly, slumped over to one side. He looked even closer, and realized that they were all corpses. Crows landed on them, picking at them.

Thor walked his horse between them and saw that these were all men of the Western Kingdom, all great warriors whom he had once trained with. His heart broke.

Amidst them, their walked a single person, walking out slowly to greet him. A woman. She was the most beautiful woman he'd ever seen, dressed in luminescent blue robes, and she walked slowly across the field, and reached out a hand to him.

"Thorgrin, my love," she said. "Come to me."

Thor squinted and realized it was Gwendolyn. He tried to ride towards her, but his horse would not move. He looked down and saw that it was stuck in the mud.

"Thorgrin," he called. "I need you."

Thor finally broke his horse free, and he charged, galloping through the fields for her.

But as he reached her, she disappeared.

Thor looked about and saw that he was no longer on a battlefield, but in a wide-open desert. Riding towards him was a sole warrior, bedecked in shining gold armor, the sun radiating behind so brightly that Thor had to squint.

They rode towards each other and came to stop but a few feet away, Thor squinting, trying to see who it was against the glare of the sun.

"Who are you?" Thor called out. "Announce yourself!"

"It is me, father," the proud warrior said. "Your son."

The warrior removed his helmet, revealing golden hair—but the light shining behind him was so fierce, Thor could not make out his features.

Thor felt humbled at the words, ashamed that he was facing him in battle.

"My son?" he asked, shocked. "How can it be?"

Thor threw his sword down to the ground and prepared to dismount, to embrace his son.

But the boy suddenly raised a long spear, cried out, and charged towards Thor, aiming to pierce it through his chest.

Thor blinked, and found himself lying on his back, tied to a rowboat, floating in a vast ocean. The huge, rolling waves bobbed him up and down, and he was exhausted, parched, as he looked up at the passing sky. As he floated he saw a steep cliff come into view, at the ocean's edge, with a castle perched at its peak; he saw a footbridge leading up to it, and at the top, looking down, he saw his mother. A shining blue light emanated from her, and she reached out a single hand.

"My Thorgrin," she said, "return to me."

Thorgrin tried to break his bonds with all his might, to reach for her. But he could not.

"I have strayed too far, mother," he said weakly.

"It is not too late," she said. "You have the power to return."

"Mother!" he screamed out, "I can't break free. My bonds are too strong!"

"You can, Thorgrin," she said. "You have the strength. You can!"

Thor struggled all his might, and this time, something was different. This time, he heard his leather bonds groan, then finally snap.

Thor reached up with his free hand, and as he did, his mother reached down for him. For the first time, he felt her hand. It carried a strength unlike any he had ever felt. There she was, her hand grasping his, pulling him up. He felt an overwhelming strength infuse his body.

He felt all his bonds breaking. He felt himself being lifted up into the sky, soaring higher and higher, for her castle, for home.

"Mother," he said, so relieved.

She smiled back.

"You are home now, my son. You are home now."

Thor opened his eyes and sat up with a start, looking all about him. Something felt different inside him. Something had changed.

Dawn was breaking, and all around him were Empire soldiers, slowly rousing, preparing for the day, for the battle ahead. Thor looked up to see Andronicus approaching him. But no longer did Thor view the Empire soldiers as colleagues; and no longer did he see Andronicus as his father. Now, he had a whole new perspective; he had a moment of clarity. He saw them all as the enemy. And he saw his father as the enemy he was.

Andronicus approached, smiling, and held out his palm. Thor looked down and saw his mother's ring.

"I promised you, my son," Andronicus said. "And I always keep my promises."

Andronicus reached down and placed the ring in Thor's palm.

As he did, Thor felt an overwhelming strength race through him. He also felt a sense of clarity. He was Thorgrin, of the Western Kingdom of the Ring. He was a member of the Legion, loyal to MacGil, and he was fighting to free the Ring. And all of these men about him, they were all the enemy.

Thor drew his sword, and he suddenly charged. Andronicus lay before him, and Thor was determined.

It was time to kill his father.

CHAPTER TWENTY FIVE

Kendrick charged down the steep slope of the Highlands in the breaking dawn, into the thick mist, red sunlight flooding the valley, Erec, Bronson and Srog beside him, and thousands of men behind them, as they all charged for the division of Empire soldiers in the valley below. Thus far, their strategy of hit-and-run had been a success: they had attacked Highlandia, wiped out a small division of Andronicus' men, and had taken shelter back in the mountains. They had been lucky, though, that Romulus had attacked when he had. Kendrick did not know if they could have won otherwise, especially with Thor fighting at Andronicus' side.

It still rattled Kendrick to the core, the image of Thor riding out to greet him in battle. It left a pit in his stomach. How could Kendrick possibly face his comrade, his brother-in-arms, in battle? What would he have done if Thor had attacked him? What had they done to change Thor?

Kendrick did not imagine he'd be able to harm Thor. Clearly, Thor was under the spell of Andronicus, of some dark force, and he was not himself. Yet at the same time, Thor was still clearly more powerful than any of his men, and Kendrick winced at the thought that he might have to face him soon enough in battle—or else risk losing his men.

For now, at least, that would not be an issue: Kendrick's men had identified a lone division of Empire troops camped on the other side of the valley, a few thousand warriors, isolated from the rest of the Empire camp. They rode now at sunrise with stealth and surprise, Kendrick's thousands of men prepared to attack them quick and hard, then retreat back into the mountains. Kendrick and his men were still outnumbered, but they feared not for greater numbers, as long as the odds were close and as long as they weren't fighting the entire Empire army at once.

Kendrick did not know how long this strategy could last. But if they could keep picking off one small division of Empire troops a time, eventually, he felt, they could win this war. When faced with an opponent greater in size and strength and numbers, sometimes stealth and cunning and retreating selectively was the most effective way to wage war, he figured.

The sound of horses' hooves reverberated in Kendrick's ear, along with the clang of armor, as they all rode, the cool morning wind in his hair and his hand tightening on the hilt of his sword. The morning mist finally lifted, revealing his men and giving away the element of surprise. But at least they had made it this far.

Kendrick and his men let out a great battle cry as they bore down, hardly a hundred yards away. The Empire men, startled, all turned, and looked up with terror at the sight and sound of them charging down the mountain. Their first impulse was to flee, and several dozen Empire soldiers on the front lines turned and ran back, in panic.

But soon they gathered themselves, as hardened Empire commanders stepped forward and rallied their men. A fighting force was quickly assembled, and stood ready to meet them.

Kendrick, Erec, Bronson, Srog and the others did not give them a chance. They charged faster, and, lances out, met them with a great clash of armor.

The sound of steel meeting steel filled the air. Cries rang out of men killing men, and bodies fell, mostly on the Empire side, the MacGil men charging down the slope of the Highlands like a sudden storm. Their momentum carried them right into the thick of the Empire camp, cutting a broad swath right through, killing men left and right as they all tried to put on their armor, to gather their weapons, to mount their horses.

Within moments, several hundred Empire troops were dead or wounded, and as Kendrick and his men continued to charge their way through, it seemed as if nothing could stop them. Kendrick felt sure they would take out this entire division and return to the mountains before the morning sun even lifted in the sky.

Suddenly, Kendrick felt his horse's legs go out from under him, and as his horse collapsed, Kendrick went diving, landing hard, face-first, on the ground. His armor clanked as he rolled and rolled.

Erec, Bronson and Srog rolled on the ground beside him. Out of breath, Kendrick turned and looked back, wondering what had happened.

Kendrick found the culprit: unbeknownst to him, the Empire men had laid out a long, studded barbed chain, and had yanked it tight, cutting out his horse's legs from under them, and sending them all crashing to the ground. The Empire men employed expert discipline. Kendrick had grown too confident in battle, and had underestimated his opponent.

A sword came down for his head, and Kendrick raised a shield just in time, as dozens of Empire men swarmed down all around him. He blocked the blows, rolled, and swung out and slashed the soldiers' legs, making them drop to the ground beside him.

Kendrick quickly gained his feet, dodging blows, using his shield as he fended off several Empire soldiers. They were closing in fast, and all around him, Erec, Bronson, Srog and others were fighting hand-to-hand, too.

Kendrick stabbed a soldier, and as he slumped over, Kendrick snatched a flail from his waist. He raised it high and wielded it in a wide circle over his head, smashing many Empire soldiers in the chest and face, knocking them back, and creating a wide perimeter around he and the other men. He bought them some breathing room.

As Kendrick fought hard, he turned and searched for his men, for reinforcements, wondering what was taking them so long. But as he looked, he saw that his men had their hands full, too: the Empire division was receiving reinforcements and troops were flooding into the valley from all sides. His men were backlogged, unable to reach him. Now the momentum was turning the other way; the tide of battle, while it looked good before, was now beginning to sway against them.

Kendrick fought with both hands, already exhausted, the odds only getting worse. On the horizon, as the mist rose further, he saw even more Empire troops, thousands more, swelling in to reinforce the others. They were far more greatly outnumbered than he thought. This was not an isolated Empire division after all, but part of a much larger battalion.

Standing there, holding his ground, he and Erec and Bronson and Srog fought with all their hearts, killing off their attackers, fighting for each other, protecting one another. But Kendrick already knew in his heart that he had made a grave mistake in coming here. They were vastly outnumbered, and the odds were getting worse. In only a short matter of time, his army would suffer its final defeat.

*

Godfrey rode before his thousands of men, Akorth and Fulton beside him, his Silesian general behind them, and thousands of

MacGils following. Godfrey had no idea why these men were following them, or why they had entrusted him at all—or why his sister Gwendolyn had, either. He was not a soldier. He was not a brave warrior, like the others. He used his wit to survive, and that was all he had.

Godfrey's ploy had worked back there, had saved them from the initial Empire attack. It had been the best gold he'd ever spent. But his luck had come to an end, and eventually, he knew, he must face battle. He could only evade for so long. And he knew that in battle, *real* battle, eventually wit would only take him so far. He would also need skills in fighting. And these he sorely lacked.

Godfrey had heart, at least. He charged forward, despite his fears, leading these men, determined to find Kendrick and Erec and the others and do what he could to help them. He knew he would probably die in this cause. But he no longer cared. He felt it was past time for him to do something in his life that was not about himself. It was time to fight in the same ways that others fought—even if it meant losing.

As he rode, Godfrey marveled at how confident all the other soldiers seemed. He himself, he had to admit, felt overwhelmed with fear. But at least he continued riding anyway, riding through it.

Godfrey crested a hill, recognizing the spot described by his informant. His spies had paid off men in Tirus' army, and these had told him about Kendrick's men being set free. He had paid off informants every step of the way, to show him where Kendrick and Erec had gone. And he had been following their trail ever since. He dearly hoped his informants had been right.

Godfrey followed the tracks of a vast army up the hill, and he wondered where they were going, and why. All this work was exhausting. He would give anything for a pint of ale now, and a warm fire to lay his feet beside.

As Godfrey crested the hilltop in the breaking sun, he was out of breath. He had ridden all night to catch up to Kendrick and Erec, and now, finally, as they reached the peak, he stopped and looked down at the valley spread out below him. His stomach fell at the sight.

There, below, were Kendrick, Erec, Bronson and Srog, with thousands of Silver and MacGils and Silesians and McClouds, all surrounded by the Empire and fighting for their lives. They were completely engulfed by Empire men, and thousands more poured in.

Godfrey sat there on his horse, breathing hard, paralyzed with fear. He was terrified. All the men he loved were about to be killed before his eyes, and what remained of their armies wiped out.

"Sire, now what?" his general asked. "We cannot attack. We are vastly outnumbered. It would be suicide."

"Let's retreat," Akorth said.

Fulton nodded vigorously.

"I agree. Let's save our own lives. We can't help them anyway."

But Godfrey would not be swayed; the old Godfrey might have cowered and slunk away. But not anymore. Now he was determined.

Godfrey looked around eagerly, desperate to figure out a way to help. He couldn't let his brother die out there; yet he also didn't want to charge into a certain death. He was desperate to find another solution.

Come on.

Godfrey summoned his wit, every ounce of his intelligence. He'd always had a knack for finding another way when others could not, for taking a step back and getting a bird's-eye view of a situation, and coming up with a solution that no one else thought of. As he studied the peaks of the Highlands, up and down, suddenly, he spotted something.

His heart raced, as suddenly, he got an idea.

Godfrey pointed.

"There!" he yelled.

Akorth and Fulton followed his finger, baffled.

"There what?" Akorth asked.

"What are you pointing to?" Fulton asked. "A rock?"

Godfrey shook his head, annoyed.

"*There!*" he said more firmly, pointing. "On that ridge!"

Akorth and Fulton squinted.

"All I see is a shepherd, my lord," his general said, "and a flock of bulls."

Godfrey smiled.

"Exactly," he replied.

Godfrey looked down the hillside to the battlefield, then looked back to the bulls at the peak.

"You're not thinking what I think you're thinking, are you?" Akorth asked Godfrey.

"There must be at least a thousand bulls there," Godfrey said. "A number of them look unhappy. They are anxious to be set free. And I intend to help them."

Godfrey looked back down at the battlefield below, the steep slope, and figured if he could set loose these bulls, if he could get them to charge down, in a rage, into the mayhem, there was no limit to the damage and confusion they would cause. It would be an enormous distraction. And that was exactly what Kendrick and his men needed at this moment.

"Madness!" the general said. "A crazy scheme. One for dreaming boys—not for military commanders!"

Godfrey turned to his general.

"I would take a dreaming boy over a military commander any day. CHARGE!" he screamed to his men.

Godfrey drew his sword and screamed as he charged, racing for the flock of bulls, sword held high, prepared to send them as his missionaries into the field of battle.

CHAPTER TWENTY SIX

Reece, O'Connor, Elden, Indra, Conven, Serna and Krog followed Centra as he navigated his way quickly through the Canyon base, their feet sticking to the muddy floor as they weaved their way between the exotic trees, orange and turquoise leaves flashing amidst the muted sunlight. Reece's feet stuck as they went, making each step an effort, and every now and again another hot spring erupted close by, spewing steam and mud into the air, small flakes of mud raining down and sticking to him. Reece's face and skin was already caked with mud, and with a salty residue that clung to everything. He felt caked in layers, felt like he needed a bath, like he was becoming part of this mud landscape and would never return.

Strange noises filled the air, continually putting Reece on edge. He thought back to their encounter with the monster, and wondered what else could be down here. If it weren't for Centra, surely they would be dead. Who'd ever heard of a monster with a heart in its foot? He looked about warily, his visibility limited between the trees and the mist, and he could not help but wonder what other dangers lurked here.

Reece thought back to the Sword, and he peered at the Canyon floor, following the ominous trail left by the Faws. The more they followed it, the more he wondered about these people, these scavengers, who took it. He wondered at their strength, being able to drag it, and wondered what they could want with it. More ominously, he wondered how powerful they were, given they had survived down here, amidst all these creatures.

"Perhaps these Faws, they'll listen to reason and give us the Sword back," O'Connor offered aloud. "After all, they know it's not theirs."

Centra snorted, shaking his head.

"The Faws are not exactly the type to listen to reason."

"Maybe we can trade them something for it," O'Connor said.

"The only thing they'd want to trade you for is your head on a stick," Centra said.

O'Connor fell silent.

"We're entering the far side of the Canyon," Centra said. "Have you noticed how many more springs there are? It's a virtual landmine. The quakes come more frequently here, too. Have you noticed the cracks in the Canyon walls? We have minor quakes…."

Reece tried to tune Centra out. Centra had not stopped talking since they had met; clearly, this man was lonely, desperate for company. All along the way, he had filled them in on every last thing about the bottom of the Canyon, from the climate to the geography to the seasons, to all the animals and insects and peoples who lived here.

Reece was growing impatient. What he wanted to know about specifically was the tribe who had taken the Sword.

"Tell us more about the Faws," Reece said, cutting Centra off.

Centra turned to him, as if surprised to be interrupted.

"What do you want to know?"

"Everything."

Centra sighed. He shook his head, as he continued walking quickly, following tracks that Reece could not decipher. Reece hoped that Centra knew where he was going. He felt the urgency of time; they had to get the Sword and return as soon as they could. His best friend's life depended on it. Descending here had been far more challenging than Reece could have ever imagined.

"The Faws are the most vicious of all creatures down here. Even the monster you fought back there would stay clear of them. They are given a lot of respect, and no one enters their territory. I always stick to my side of the Canyon, and I never enter their territory when hunting."

"Are they that fierce?" Elden asked.

"Not individually," Centra said. "But collectively, yes. You see, they stick together, like bees, and they fight as one. That is their great strength. They are all in synchronicity. And there are so many of them. They descend on something together, and that's it. It's finished."

"They are not large and strong then?" O'Connor asked.

Centra laughed.

"No. Quite the opposite. Quite small, indeed. But do not underestimate your opponent by his appearance. Isn't that the first law of battle?"

There came a moaning, and Reece turned and saw Krog, being carried between Elden and O'Connor, crying out in pain. He slumped down, and they lay him down in the mud. He seemed delirious.

"Leave me," he said. "I can't go on."

Reece came over and knelt by his side, examining him. He was sweating profusely, and very pale. Reece leaned over and placed a hand on his head, and he was burning to the touch.

"We don't leave anyone behind," Reece said. "I told you that already."

Krog scowled back.

"I would leave you if it were me," Krog answered.

"I'm not you," Reece replied.

Indra came and stood over him.

"Leave him here, if he wants," she said coldly. "I, for one, can do without him."

"No one gets left behind," Reece repeated.

"Do you forget how he has acted? He has defied us at every turn," she said. "Not to mention he will slow us down and get in our way."

"No one," Reece repeated emphatically. "I don't care who they are or what they've done. It is not about them; it is about us. Our code of honor. If we lose that, we lose it all."

Indra relented as the group fell silent, looking down at Krog.

"Well I won't go on," Krog said, writhing. "I can't."

"It's a nasty wound, is it?" Centra asked, coming over.

He pushed Reece aside and kneeled before Krog. He pulled back the cloth on Krog's calf, revealing a deep, black, festering wound, left from the impact of the tree. He recoiled.

"Nasty indeed," Centra said. "He'll be dead in a day at this rate. You should have told me. All he needs is Sulfur Mud. It won't heal him entirely, but it will take away the pain and will make it much better. Get him to his feet, and follow me."

"Is it out of the way?" Indra asked.

"Not by much," Centra said, looking back and forth between Reece and Indra, unsure.

"Take us there," Reece ordered.

They followed Centra as he changed direction, weaving in and out of the trees, up and down rolling hills, until finally they arrived at a large mound of bubbling mud. It was hissing, and a mist was rising from it.

Centra stepped close, reached over, grabbed a scoop of mud, and applied it as a balm on Krog's leg.

Krog immediately perked up. His eyes opened wide in surprise, and within moments, he went from being slumped over between the others to standing upright on his own. He even took a step on his own. Then another. He was limping, but he was walking. And judging from the smile on his face, he was no longer in pain.

"How did you do that?" Krog asked.

"The mud won't last long," Centra said. "But long enough to get you out of here. When its effects wear off, you'll be worse than before. Let's just hope we can find you all this Sword and get you out of here quickly."

They all turned and followed Centra as he weaved back in and out of the mud hills, picking up his old trail.

As Reece walked, Krog walked up beside him, limping.

"You helped me," Krog said. "Why?"

"Why?" Reece asked. "Why wouldn't I?"

"You're a strange one," Krog said. "I'm not sure if I like you or not. I wish you would have left me back there. Then it would have been easier to hate you."

Reece furrowed his brow, confused.

"Are you trying to thank me?" Reece asked.

"I guess in my own way, I am," Krog said. "But that doesn't mean I like you."

Reece shook his head, not understanding Krog's way of thought at all.

"Well, you're welcome," Reece said, ending their odd conversation.

Reece saw the darkening sky all around them, and he began to worry. What would happen if they had to make camp down here? Would they be able to track down the Faws in the dark?

"It's just beyond that hill!" Centra called out excitedly.

They all turned and looked.

"You can hear the buzzing from here," Centra continued. "That's the main camp of the Faws. And that's where they took the Sword: see the trail?"

They all crowded around, and Reece indeed saw the trail, rising up the hill of mud. He heard the buzzing, too. It sounded like an endless swarm of bees.

"But I tell you, it makes no sense to try to breach their territory," Centra continued. "They have many tricks. They don't fight fairly. You cannot win."

"We will fight any foe who stands in our way," Reece said confidently. "If you are concerned, you can leave us now. And we thank you for your help."

Centra shook his head.

"Foolish to the last," he said. He smiled. "That's what I like to hear. Finally, someone as crazy as me. Follow me."

They all followed Centra up the large hill, each of them slipping and sliding as they went, Reece's palms covered in mud. Just as they were out of breath, Reece's stomach aching from the effort and from lack of food, they reached the top.

Reece stood there with the others and looked down at the sight before him in wonder. Below, in a broad valley of mud, was the camp of the Faws. There were thousands of them, short and skinny orange creatures, perhaps three feet high, with three long, skinny fingers and bright green eyes. Their faces were shaped in wide smiles, their jagged teeth showing. They milled about quickly, all busy, carrying things with their hands, like a worker mill of ants.

Their village was populated with small, primitive huts, made of the leaves of these strange trees, orange and turquoise. In the center of their village was a hole in the earth, perhaps ten yards in diameter, and inside it, bubbling up, was molten fire. It hissed and bubbled ominously, illuminating the whole village. Clearly their entire village revolved around this strange hole of molten fire.

"What is it?" Reece asked.

"They worship it," Centra said. "They are the people of the lava. They believe that is why their skin is orange. They pray to the lava as if it were a god. Every day they sacrifice another person in it. It's their favorite way to kill their enemies."

Reece looked closely, and there, atop a large mound, near the lava, sat the boulder. Dozens of Faws knelt around it, humming and praying, bowing to it. They hummed and worshipped it, as if it were a god. And there sat the Sword, lodged in it, shining.

Reece's heart quickened as he saw it.

"Our Sword," he gasped.

"You waste your energy to look at it," Centra said. "It's as gone from you as if it were in another world. You'll never get it back. Once the Faws have something, it is theirs."

Centra turned to Reece and grasped his wrist, his expression earnest.

"I tell you, turn back now."

There came the sudden ring of a sword being drawn, and Reece turned to see Conven, standing there, sword in hand, staring down at the village defiantly.

Reece turned and looked at Centra.

"We turn back for no one, my friend."

Reece drew his sword, too, and as soon as he did, suddenly, everything changed.

There came the sound of gushing water, and Reece felt his feet wobble, as he looked down.

"MUDSLIDE!" Centra yelled, the first to react, diving to jump out of the way.

But he was not quick enough.

Reece felt his legs being knocked out from under him, and he screamed, as did all the others, as they were suddenly caught up in a great gushing river of mud, sending them flying down the hill, straight down into the village, faster than he could react—and right towards the Faws.

As Reece looked straight ahead, he saw dozens of Faws appear, carrying a huge net. It was then that Reece realized that they had set the mudslide off, that they had been watching them the whole time, that they had walked right into a trap. And that he had underestimated the enemy. He should have listened to Centra all along.

It was too late now. He went sliding at full speed with the others, right into the center of the camp, and braced himself as the huge net swallowed them all.

CHAPTER TWENTY SEVEN

Thor lunged for Andronicus, sword drawn, aiming to kill him.

Andronicus' eyes opened wide in surprise; clearly he had not been expecting this from his son. Yet his reflexes kicked in, and as Thor charged, Andronicus dodged, stepping out of the way right before the sword could impale him.

Thorgrin continued charging, right into the crowd of unsuspecting Empire soldiers, killing them left and right with a great battle cry. He slashed and stabbed one after the other, and soon, the bodies piled up, and soldiers ran to get out of his way.

Chaos ensued in the camp. Empire soldiers, confused, rushed to grab weapons, to don armor, to counter-attack. But they were no match for Thor. Thor was a thing of beauty, a one-man killing machine.

"KILL HIM!" Rafi screamed to Andronicus. "Why do you just stand there?"

But Andronicus stood there, frozen, loathe to kill his son. For the first time in his life, he was unsure what to do.

Rafi, grunting in frustration, stepped forward himself. He threw back his hood, reached out, and raised both palms for Thorgrin.

A scarlet light shot from his hand and swirled around Thor, embracing him. Rafi screamed, shaking his hands violently, and the light grew thicker and thicker.

Finally, Thor, immersed in the circle of light, slowed down his killing, then stopped and sank to his knees. He reached up for his head, screaming, then slumped down and lay there, unconscious.

Andronicus came and stood over him, Rafi beside him. Despite everything, it pained him to see his son lying there.

"You kept him alive?" Andronicus asked. It was more of a warning than a question.

"Reluctantly," Rafi answered.

"Is he back on our side?" Andronicus asked, hopefully.

"For now," Rafi said. "There was a lapse in his will. He has a very strong will, stronger than I have ever encountered. I don't know how long I can control him. It is dangerous to keep him alive. I have told you this already. You must kill him now."

Andronicus shook his head.

"He is back to our side," he said, "he will not lapse again."

Rafi scowled.

"Your weakness for your son is going to get us all killed. I warn you: if you do not kill him yourself, then someday, I will."

Andronicus turned to Rafi and reddened.

"I care not what power you wield," he said. "Speak to me this way again, and I myself will cast you down to the lowest ring of hell."

Rafi turned and stormed off.

Andronicus, riled, stood over his son, looked down at him and wondered. Was Thor's love for him real? Or was it due to Rafi's spell?

"Shall we shackle him, my lord?" an Empire general asked, coming up, holding shackles.

Andronicus shoved him hard in the chest, knocking him back.

"Kill him," Andronicus ordered, pointing to his general.

Several Empire soldiers came running over and dragged away the Empire general, who stared back, confused.

Andronicus knelt down, picked up his son, and carried him gently in his arms.

"It is okay, Thornicus," he said softly, as he carried him off. "You are with your father again now."

Andronicus would carry him to the finest tent and give him the finest sleeping quarters. He was certain Rafi's spell would hold this time. Tomorrow would be the final battle with Thor's people, and Andronicus needed him. Once Thor had killed his own, Andronicus was certain, there would be no turning back.

Thor would be his forever.

CHAPTER TWENTY EIGHT

Kendrick raised his shield and dropped to one knee, as blow after blow rained down upon him. He stood in the thick of the battle, completely surrounded by Empire men, three of them, large brutes, charging at him, and slamming down at his shield with their battle axes and hammers. The ring of metal reverberated in his ears, and his wrists were bruised as he held back the blows, pouring down, one after the other. They were fierce, and his arms shook.

Kendrick defeated many combatants here today, but his men were too outnumbered by the fresh Empire reinforcements. At this point, he was just holding on for dear life; he barely had the strength to parry. He knew he would not be able to last much longer.

Not far away, Erec, Bronson and Srog fought brilliantly, too, yet they were in the same predicament: all of them were getting tired, increasingly surrounded by Empire men, unable to catch their momentum and fight back. They were now all just defending, fighting for survival.

All around Kendrick men were beginning to fall, their screams ringing out, MacGils, Silver, Silesians, and McClouds. The tide of battle had turned against them, and Kendrick momentarily closed his eyes, sweat dripping into them, and felt his moments were numbered. He knew he should be grateful: he had, at least, got his wish: he would die fighting, on his feet, as a true warrior, defending his homeland. It would be a noble death, one that any warrior would wish for.

As Kendrick held back the blows, he thought he heard a distant noise; at first he thought he was imagining it. It sounded like a distant rumbling, like a herd of horses charging.

Soon, it grew more intense. The ground began to tremble, then to shake. And then, there came the screams of men. But not his men— Empire men. All around him, Empire soldiers began to turn and flee. Soon, the blows stopped raining down on Kendrick, as the men fighting him turned and ran.

Kendrick was confused. He turned to see what the commotion was, and as he looked up at the mountainside, he saw a sight that he would never forget for as long as he lived. He blinked several times, trying to comprehend it.

There, charging down the steep mountainside, were at least a thousand bulls, huge red animals, racing down, livid with rage, and heading right into the thick of Empire soldiers. They gored men left and right with their horns, and the battlefield turned red with blood. All of the Empire soldiers on the outskirts of the battlefield, to their bad fortune, were killed by the animals.

Yet still more animals charged down, a never-ending stream, trampling men, rushing deeper and deeper into the field of battle, devouring as many soldiers as they could. Some of his own men fell, too, but, being so outnumbered, it was mostly Empire.

Kendrick could hardly believe it: of all the crazy things he had seen in battle, this had to be the craziest. They had all been given a second chance.

As Kendrick looked up into the rising sun, he saw another sight which astounded him, even more so: there, leading the charge of thousands of soldiers, was none other than his younger brother, Godfrey, flanked by Akorth and Fulton. They rode clumsily, like warriors unused to battle, yet still they rode, racing down the slope, following the bulls, and bringing thousands of men with them.

Kendrick smiled wide. His brother had arrived after all.

This was the opportunity Kendrick had been waiting for, and he was determined to seize it. Kendrick, along with Erec, Bronson and Srog, turned and charged for the Empire, reinvigorated, screaming a great battle cry.

Behind him his men rallied, the tide of battle changing yet again, as they all rushed forward, into the thick of the fleeing Empire soldiers, and fought back, killing hundreds, while doing their best to dodge the bulls. Godfrey's men joined the fray, and they all fought together, pushing back the Empire men.

They chased them all the way through the valley, slaughtering men left and right. Soon, they had managed to even the odds, no longer so outnumbered as they were before. Before long they were clearly winning, outnumbering even the remaining Empire men.

Kendrick's heart pounded with joy as he realized they were going to win this battle after all, thanks to Godfrey and his bulls. He shook his head as he fought, smiling to himself. Leave it up to his younger brother to find some crafty way to win this war.

As they chased the Empire men around a bend, finishing off the remnants, a new vista opened up, and Kendrick suddenly stopped short, along with all the others, at what he saw.

There, on the horizon, riding to face them in battle, was yet another division of Empire men. Many thousands more than Kendrick had.

Yet that was not what deterred him. What made him stop, made him freeze in his tracks, was the person leading the charge.

There, riding out front, sword held high, was one of the men he cared for most in the world: Thorgrin.

Kendrick's greatest fear had come true: their time to meet in battle had come.

CHAPTER TWENTY NINE

Gwendolyn walked in awe through the Valley of Trapped Souls, the endless maze of frozen bodies, Alistair, Steffen, and Aberthol beside her, Krohn at her feet, snarling. They were all on edge. It was the most eerie and desolate landscape that Gwen had ever entered. Every twenty feet or so another ice capsule protruded from the earth, each perhaps ten feet high, and just wide enough to contain a body. They were translucent, and inside each Gwen saw a frozen body, staring out with an expression of agony.

"What is this place?" Steffen asked.

"They are all trapped souls," Aberthol remarked. "Destined to live out the rest of their days here." Aberthol's voice shook with exhaustion as he walked, leaning on his staff, the sound of it clicking on the ice floor the only thing to break the silence. "It appears in many of the ancient books. I never knew it really existed. And I never thought to lay eyes upon it in my lifetime. Then again, I never thought I'd take a journey such as this at my age."

"But who are these people?" Steffen pressed.

"This place is a sort of purgatory," Aberthol said, "a place where those of the magic race are brought to be trapped. Punished. To serve out their sentence."

"For how long?" Alistair asked, looking up in wonder. She examined one face, of a young girl, trapped behind the ice, face pressed up against it in an expression of sadness.

"For some, it could be centuries," Aberthol replied. "Their experience of time is different than ours."

"What did Argon do to deserve such a sentence?" Steffen asked.

Gwendolyn felt overwhelmed by guilt as she pondered the question. She had been thinking the same exact thing, thinking how guilty she felt for Argon's being here on her account. And how humbled with gratitude she was to imagine that he would risk all of it, would risk being put in this place, to save her life.

"He violated the sacred law," Gwen said softly to the others. "He interfered in human affairs to help me. He saved my life. Seeing this, I wish he hadn't. I would have rather died on the battlefield that day than to see him suffer this way."

"Do not blame yourself," Alistair said, placing a hand on her shoulder. "Remember, Argon had his own destiny, too. Maybe it was his destiny to help you."

Gwen had never considered that, and Alistair's words, as always, provided her a sense of solace. Still, she felt ridden with guilt, and determined to find him—and free him. She would make wrongs right, no matter what she had to do.

"He will not be here forever," Gwendolyn said back firmly. "What's done can be undone."

Gwen turned to Aberthol.

"Can't it?" she asked, hopeful. "Can't trapped souls be freed?"

Aberthol sighed, and looked down grimly.

"I've never heard of anyone being freed from the Valley of Souls," he said. "I don't know how it's possible. I don't even know how you are going to find him."

Gwendolyn was wondering the same thing as they all marched through the valley, larger than any cemetery she'd ever seen, tens of thousands of frozen figures before them, like monuments to some other world. It was eerie and haunting. A gale of wind rushed through, freezing her to the bone, and she pulled her furs tighter.

Gwen could not even see where the valley ended, and it could take months to walk through this land. She was beginning to feel hopeless. She had no idea how they would ever find Argon here.

Please, father, she prayed silently. *Please help me.*

Gwen thought of her dad, King MacGil, of how much he'd loved her, of how much she'd missed him. She'd never felt more alone. She wished he could be by her side, that he could guide her again, could help her. Why had he had to leave her alone with all of this? Why couldn't he just be there to help her now?

Gwen heard a screech, high up in the sky, and she looked up with surprise to see a lone bird, circling. At first she could not see it well, amidst the clouds; but then it lowered, and screeched again, and her heart soared as she recognized it: her father's bird. Estopheles.

Estopheles dove down low, screeching, circling them. She dove down low, then rose up, circling again and again, and Gwendolyn felt she was trying to give them a message. She flew off to one side, diving and rising, spreading her wings, and Gwendolyn felt more and more certain she was trying to tell them something. She felt that Estopheles was trying to lead them somewhere.

Gwen had a thrill as she realized: perhaps her prayers had been answered. Perhaps she was leading them to Argon.

"She is telling us something," Gwendolyn said to the others. "We must follow her."

Gwendolyn turned and headed off in another direction, following her.

She marched quickly through the valley, and the others fell in behind her. She looked up, watching the sky, weaving her way between the ice capsules, all the trapped souls. She looked up at the faces, the bodies as she went, each capsule holding a more exotic creature. Not all were human. Some of them were of races she had never seen. There were men and women, young and old, in cloaks and robes. She wondered what they had all done to be sentenced and imprisoned here. It was like a vast army of the undead. In some ways, though, it was worse than dying. Here, they all seemed stuck in an awful state—not alive, and not dead, either.

Gwendolyn walked and walked, the cold so intense it was freezing her to the bone. She was feeling herself slowing down, sick from hunger, from exhaustion. Estopheles flew and flew, sometimes going out of sight, and Gwen began to wonder if she were imagining it all, if she were being led to the right place.

She wondered if this would ever end. She felt an intense pain in her stomach, felt her baby, Thor's baby, turning over again and again, and wondered what would become of them. She had a vision of herself collapsing, being frozen in the ice, and never rising again, never being found.

Estopheles suddenly screeched, snapping her out of it, and dove straight down, into a patch of ice around the bend, perhaps a hundred yards away. She landed atop of a sole ice capsule, turned to Gwen and screeched.

Gwendolyn summoned her last bit of energy, walking towards it as quickly as she could, when suddenly she dropped to her knees in pain, and felt an awful twinge in her stomach. She cried out in agony, barely able to catch her breath as an intense pain shot through her. She breathed and breathed, and felt like crying, more so for her baby than for herself. She prayed he was okay.

Gwen felt a comforting hand beneath each of her arms, and looked over to see Alistair helping her up on one side, and Steffen on the other. Aberthol was huffing to catch up himself, several feet behind. Krohn came over, and licked her face, whining.

Clearly, this trek had taken a tremendous toll on her, on all of them. They all looked more dead than alive. And Gwendolyn felt such pain, she almost wished she were dead.

"Are you okay, my lady?" Alistair asked.

Gwendolyn held onto her tight, waiting for the pain to pass, to be able to breathe again. Finally, slowly, it did.

Alistair draped one arm over her shoulder, and they all began to walk again.

As Gwendolyn took one step after the next, made her way through the fields, slowly the pain subsided. She looked up and saw Estopheles on the horizon, and was determined to get there.

Finally, weaving their way between the capsules, they reached the one that Estopheles was perched on. She sat up there proudly, spreading her wings, screeching down at them.

Gwendolyn let her eyes fall, her heart pounding with anticipation, and her heart raced as she saw who was trapped inside.

Standing there, inside the ice, eyes closed, hands at his sides, was Argon.

Gwen could hardly breathe. She had found him.

Gwen stepped closer, until she was standing a foot away, and slowly she reached out with her palm and touched the ice. She felt the ice cold energy rush through her.

A tear rolled down her cheek as she looked up and stared into Argon's closed eyes, at his frozen body. Argon, one of the most powerful people she had ever encountered. Advisor to kings for centuries. Now, relegated to this. Gwen felt horrible to see him like this, like a trapped animal—and all on her account.

"Argon," she called out. "Answer me."

Gwen's voice was filled with grief. As she cried, she no longer knew if it was for Argon, or her unborn son, or her father, or Thorgrin, or herself. Grief engulfed her and she could no longer think clearly.

Argon did not answer. He did not even move. He seemed frozen forever.

"You must come back to us," she said.

Still he did not reply. He just stood there, frozen, as if lost in another world.

"Argon, I need you!" she called out, more desperate. "The Ring needs you. Thorgrin needs you. Please. Talk to me."

Gwendolyn pressed her face up against the ice, clutched it with both hands, and as she did, she felt her baby turning again and again.

Yet still, nothing happened. It seemed Argon was lost to her forever. Had she made a mistake to come here?

Gwen, determined, stepped back and drew her sword from her belt. She raised it high and slashed at the ice with all her might, determined to free him.

But it merely bounced off harmlessly, the ice not even chipped.

Steffen, following her cue, stepped forward and fired arrows at it. But these all bounced off harmlessly, too.

Gwendolyn turned to Alistair, desperate.

"Do something," she pleaded. "You are a druid. You have power. I've *seen* your power."

"What would you have me do?" she asked.

"Break the capsule. Melt the ice. Do something!"

Alistair stepped forward, closed her eyes, and held out her palm. She muttered something in a language Gwendolyn did not understand, with a low humming noise, and aimed her palm at the ice.

A yellow light streamed from her palm, for the ice capsule.

But to Gwen's surprise it bounced back, and the light soon disappeared.

Alistair pulled her hand back, as if stung.

"I'm sorry," Alistair said. "These are forces more powerful than I've ever seen. They are far greater than I."

Gwen stood there, staring, crushed. She had come all this way for nothing. There was nothing more she could do. Argon was trapped forever. And she would never be able to free Thor.

Estopheles screeched, flapped her wings, and took off into the sky. Soon, she disappeared, too.

Gwen felt her whole life slipping away from her.

Gwen, weak with exhaustion, at the end of her rope, dropped to her knees before the ice capsule. She closed her eyes and prayed.

God, if you hear me, I pray to you. Not to Argon. Not to the land. Not to the sky. Not to many gods. But to you, and you alone. There is only one god, and I turn to you now, in my time of need. I pray to, I beg you, release Argon. You can take me instead. Just release Argon. And save Thorgrin.

Gwendolyn knelt there, with her eyes closed, very quiet and still, trembling. The land was very still and quiet, nothing but the howling of the wind passing through.

Then, slowly, she began to hear a faint voice inside her head.

Gwendolyn, God has heard you.

It was Argon's voice.

Gwen opened her eyes and looked back at Argon. He remained there, frozen, unmoving, eyes closed.

"Did you hear that?" Gwen asked Alistair.

"Here what?" Alistair said.

Gwen realized that no one else had heard it. It was a voice just for her. Was she losing her mind? Or was it real?

Gwen leaned her face and hands against the ice, closed her eyes and listened.

I am lost in another world now, Argon said to her. *I can be free, but only for a great price. It is not your life that will be the price. But the life of someone very close to you. Either the life of your husband-to-be, or the life of your son. Who do you choose?*

Gwendolyn began to sob, overwhelmed with grief.

"How can I make such a choice?" she called back.

All things come with a sacrifice.

Gwen closed her eyes, crying, and slowly, she became very quiet and still. She had to choose. She *had* to.

Inside, she made her choice. As agonizing as it was, she answered quietly, in her own mind.

There came a sudden cracking noise, and Gwen opened her eyes and looked up in shock.

She stood and stepped back, as the ice she had been leaning on began to crack in her hands. The ice capsule began to crack, in a hundred places, all around Argon. Soon, it shattered, and fell to the floor.

Gwen stood there, speechless as she watched. They all stepped back in awe, as the cracking grew louder.

Soon, the ice was gone. Nothing stood between her and Argon, who stood there, hands at his sides, perfectly still.

His eyes flew open. He stared back at her, with a light more intense than any she had ever seen. It was like staring at the sun.

Argon had returned. She could not believe it.

Argon was alive.

CHAPTER THIRTY

Godfrey charged into battle with a great battle cry, Akorth and Fulton beside him, thousands of his men close behind. He rode recklessly into the heart of danger, following the bulls, and Kendrick, Erec, Bronson and Srog, determined to assist them. Godfrey's heart thumped with fear, but he was proud of himself for not turning back. He had never felt so afraid of his life; everything around him became a blur, and he could taste his own sweat as it rolled down his cheek.

If this was what battle felt like, he hated it. He never wanted to experience it again. To him it felt like a controlled state of panic. His hands shook as he raised a sword with one hand and charged for the enemy, screaming more to cover up his own fear. Why did men put themselves through this? he wondered. He would so much rather be back at home, drinking ale, chasing women and making fun of other warriors who wasted their days on the battlefield.

Yet despite it all, here he was. He rode alongside them all, headlong into a whirlwind of chaos, expecting at any moment to be knocked off his horse and killed. For once in his life, he did not care. For once in his life, he felt he was part of something bigger than himself, bigger than his fears. For once, he really let himself go. He was being overcome by a sense of abandon, and it was carrying him through.

Godfrey, dodging bulls, rounded the bend, and as he did, his fear intensified, as a huge division of Empire men appeared before him, charging at a speed which was blinding to him. He gulped. Godfrey had done his job well in releasing the bulls, and he was surprised his crazy plan had worked as well as it had. But now that he saw this new Empire division approaching, he felt it was all for nothing. They were about to die anyway, at the hands of this vastly superior force, that much was clear.

Scaring him most of all was the sight of the person leading the charge. It made his knees go weak. There, right before him, was a man he had thought of as a brother. Thorgrin. Godfrey could not believe it: Thor was charging right for them. He looked possessed, bigger and stronger than ever, charging for them with blinding force, with a sword that Godfrey did not recognize. It had the markings of the

Empire, and Thor wielded it as if it were alive. He rode as if borne on wings of lightning.

Godfrey braced himself, as he realized he was right in Thor's path. Why he, of all people?

"Thor!" Godfrey screamed out as they got closer, hoping maybe Thor recognize them, would lower his arms, would turn some other way.

But it did not work. Thor's eyes looked possessed, and he charged right for him.

Godfrey raised his shield with both hands, bracing himself for an awful blow.

Thor bore down on him and raised his sword high, scowling, and Godfrey knew he was finished.

Godfrey became so nervous that he flinched in advance, and accidentally twisted and slid sideways, beginning an awkward fall off his horse.

That accidental twist saved him. As Thor swung his sword, it just missed Godfrey, the sword connecting with Godfrey's shield instead of his head. It impacted with a great clang, and sent Godfrey falling off his horse for good.

Godfrey went flying off his horse and landed on the ground with a hard thud, the wind knocked out of him, rolling in the dirt, gasping for breath, his head ringing. He rolled and rolled, and finally stopped and lifted his head.

All around him was the stampede of a thousand horses, riding every which way—and as he raised his chin, the last thing he saw was a horse's hoof, coming right down for his forehead and knocking him out for good.

*

Andronicus was pleased to watch Thornicus back to his old self, fighting with abandon, leading the charge and cutting his way through the field of his fellow countrymen. On the front lines of those riding out to meet him were hundreds of McClouds, foolish enough to think they could defeat his son.

Thor wielded his weapon like a thing of fury, killing a half dozen men in a single stroke. The field ran red with the blood of the Ring, the McClouds falling at Thor's feet.

Andronicus smiled, satisfied—and then charged into the fray himself.

Wielding a three-headed flail, Andronicus swung its long chain and found target after target, smashing the enemy, knocking off heads left and right. He was too tall, too strong, too fast for all of them, and he cut a path of death right through. He grinned wide, taking it all in. He hadn't had this much fun in he didn't know how long. As Andronicus fought with abandon, he took satisfaction in knowing that he faced the last remnant of the Ring's forces; after this battle, the Ring would finally be his.

Andronicus spotted one of their leaders—Kendrick—charging for him fearlessly. This warrior was reckless indeed if he thought he could take on the Great Andronicus. Andronicus screamed and kicked his horse, and men parted as the two great warriors charged each other in an open clearing.

Andronicus swung his flail for Kendrick's head, expecting to finish him off. But he was surprised to discover that Kendrick was not like the others he'd fought: he was faster, more agile. He ducked Andronicus' blow, then parried with his sword, so fast that he even managed to slice Andronicus's forearm.

Andronicus screamed out, more in surprise than pain. He had not been bested in battle in a very long time.

But the pain only made him focus. He had been over-confident, and he now realized that Kendrick was unlike the others.

Andronicus wielded his flail, swinging it around, aiming low this time, for Kendrick's horse.

The metal studded ball impacted on Kendrick's horse's head, making it stumble.

Kendrick, caught off guard, did not see it coming, and as he leaned forward, trying to steady his horse, Andronicus lunged forward with a hidden dagger at the end of his gauntlet, and sliced Kendrick across the chest.

Kendrick cried out, but spun around with his shield and smashed Andronicus across the face, something Andronicus had not anticipated.

Andronicus stumbled back; in the same motion he reached over, grabbed a short spear he had hidden in his saddle, spun and hurled it at Kendrick.

The spear embedded itself in Kendrick's shoulder, and Kendrick screamed out, grabbing for it.

Andronicus leaned forward and smashed Kendrick with his shield with all his might, hitting his jaw and knocking him off his horse, spear in his shoulder.

Kendrick landed on the ground hard, immobile, and his horse went down with him. Andronicus felt more satisfaction than he had in years.

Andronicus circled around, preparing to finish him off. But as he raised his spear high, he was attacked by several of Kendrick's men, and soon distracted fighting them. Out of the corner of his eye, he saw Kendrick roll away, and head off to another battle.

Another time, Andronicus told himself. Kendrick would, sooner or later, die by his hand.

*

Bronson fought with all he had, choosing to forego his shield and instead wielding a sword with his good hand. He fought as best he could with one hand, and with his other, he wielded a flail, gripping onto it with the hook on his stub. He fought like a man possessed, doing his best to defend the Ring. He rode forward, fighting valiantly beside Srog, the two of them back to back, as they felled dozens of Empire men in each direction.

"BRONSON!" screamed out a voice.

Bronson recognized that voice anywhere. It sent a chill through his spine.

He turned and saw, amidst a group of Empire soldiers, his nemesis. His father. McCloud. The monster. The man who had taken his hand from him. The man he hated more than anything in life.

Bronson screamed and kicked his horse and charged for his father. McCloud charged back, like a demon possessed, missing one eye, his face disfigured, the emblem of the Empire burned into it. He had become a hideous creature, even more hideous than he had been.

Here they were, Bronson thought, father and son, finally facing off, finally embracing the inevitable. It was a day Bronson had long been waiting for. He would wipe out his father's name if he could. And if not, he would at least send his father to hell. It was the vengeance he'd contemplated every day as he looked down and saw his stump for a hand.

"FATHER!" Bronson screamed back.

Bronson charged with a vengeance, raising his sword high, as his father let out a cry to match his own.

The two met in the middle of an open clearing, Empire soldiers parting, and McCloud swung his battle axe, with both hands, shrieking, aiming to take off his son's head.

Bronson ducked at the last second, swung around with his flail, and managed to smash his father in the back of the head.

McCloud stumbled and fell from his horse.

Bronson wasted no time: he circled around and jumped off his, facing his father on foot, as his father slowly stood, wobbly, disoriented. Bronson brought his sword down with one hand, and McCloud raised his shield and blocked it. But Bronson slashed again and again, eventually knocking his father's shield from his grasp. Then he leaned back and kicked him.

His father stumbled and landed on his back, hurt, slow to get up.

Bronson stood over him, breathing hard, and stepped up and placed one foot on his father's throat.

McCloud gasped for air, and Bronson raised the point of his sword and held it to his father's wrist.

"You took my hand, father," Bronson said. "I should take yours. In fact, I should kill you." Bronson sighed. "But I will not sink so low. I have more honor than you. I will instead take you, unharmed, as my prisoner. Do you yield?"

McCloud struggled, gasping for air, then finally nodded yes.

Bronson slowly removed the tip of his sword from McCloud's wrist.

"Turn over and put your hands behind your back," Bronson commanded.

McCloud did so, and as he did, Bronson reached down to clasp his father, removing his extra set of shackles at his waist.

But as he reached down, McCloud suddenly spun, grabbed a handful of dirt, threw it in Bronson's eyes.

Bronson shrieked, raising his hands to his eyes and dropping his shackles. McCloud swung around and elbowed Bronson in the groin as hard as he could.

Bronson dropped to the ground, in agony.

McCloud stood over him, grabbing him by the hair on the back of his head.

"It's good to see you again, son," McCloud said.

McCloud raised his knee, and lowered Bronson's face, and a crack split the air as he broke his son's nose.

Bronson tasted blood, and the last thing he saw was the ground coming up fast, too fast, to greet him.

*

Thor charged through the battlefield, unstoppable, killing scores of McClouds who rode out to attack his father. He cut through them, faster than any of them could react, determined to protect him. That was all that mattered now. Andronicus—and crushing all of these opponents in the Ring.

Thor could not stop himself. He felt possessed, in the control of a power greater than he. His sword practically swung itself.

Thor looked over and saw his father, not far away, knock Kendrick off his horse—and for the first time, Thor blinked. For a brief moment, some long-lost part of him stirred inside; for a flash, a part of him recognized Kendrick. He could not remember from where. For just a moment, a part of him was confused about who he was fighting for.

But then Thor felt a bolt of energy, and he turned to see Rafi, riding close behind, raising his fingers in his direction. Thor felt an intense wave of energy engulf him, making it impossible to think. He felt a titanic struggle occurring within him for control, for free will. And then he felt himself subsumed by a fog.

As Thor looked back to Kendrick, he no longer recognized him. He was just another one of his father's endless opponents, of these rebels who would not cede the Ring.

There came a fierce battle cry, one different than the others, and Thor turned to see a warrior charging for him. Other soldiers parted ways, creating a wide clearing for them, and the knight stopped before Thor and faced him. There came a momentary lull in the battle, as others turned to watch. Clearly, this knight, whomever he was, was an important person on the MacGil side.

"Thorgrin. It is I, Erec!" boomed the knight, sitting proudly on his horse. "You are not yourself. I do not want to fight you. I ask you to lay down your arms. Lay down your arms and join our cause!"

Thor felt himself flush with rage. Who was this stranger to tell him what to do?

"I lay down my arms for no one!" Thor yelled back, defiant.

Thor wasted no time: he charged forward, raised his sword high, and there came a clash of swords, as he and Erec sparred furiously, back and forth, going blow for blow, neither gaining an inch.

Finally, Thor dodged one of Erec's blows and then dove from his horse and tackled him to the ground.

The two of them rolled on the ground, wrestling, neither gaining the advantage. Finally, Thor rolled out from under him and they gained their feet again.

They faced each other, and a wide clearing opened around them, all the other warriors stopping to watch.

"Thorgrin, I implore you!" Erec called out, breathing hard, blood on his lip. "It is I, Erec!"

Thor screamed and charged, sword raised high. Their swords clashed as they fought hand-to-hand, going blow for blow, shield striking sword striking shield, back and forth, perfectly matched. Neither could gain the advantage.

Thor was surprised by this knight's power and agility; he had never encountered anyone like him.

"It is I, Erec!" he said, up close, groaning, as their swords met and locked. "You know me, Thorgrin."

Thor grunted, scowling.

"My name is Thornicus!" Thor yelled, unlocking his sword.

They jabbed and slashed and parried, back and forth, until Thor's arms were growing tired, neither gaining an inch.

"You were my squire once, Thorgrin," Erec said. "I helped train you. I would do anything for you. Anything. Thorgrin, it is I, Erec."

Thor momentarily paused, something in his words striking a chord. For a passing moment he was confused, voices in his head struggling with each other, as Thor tried to understand, to know where he was, who he was. Who was this man he was fighting?

"Erec?" Thor asked.

Suddenly Rafi appeared beside Thor, and he let out an awful gurgling noise from the back of his throat as he raised his hands and directed them towards Thor.

Thor felt himself engulfed in an awful energy, and a desperate rage overcame him as he turned and set his sights on Erec.

This time, he did not recognize Erec. Not at all. He was a foe, and nothing more.

Thor raised his sword high and charged, blood in his eyes, determined this time to wipe this man off the face of the earth.

CHAPTER THIRTY ONE

Romulus galloped across the countryside, heading east, away from all the soldiers, away from the entire Empire army. Luanda was seated on the front of the horse, and she still struggled, despite his muscular arms wrapped around tight around her waist. He was surprised at her strength. Even with the ropes binding her, even with his huge arms, he had a hard time keeping her still. She was like a bucking horse. She wanted desperately to be free—but he could not let her.

Romulus rode the horse ever faster, kicking it until it protested in pain, knowing he had to make the Eastern Crossing, get back to the other side and bring Luanda with him. His magic cloak lay at the ready at his waist.

Romulus was still smarting from his defeat at the hand of Andronicus's men, something he had never anticipated. He had been sure he would take Andronicus by surprise and take over the Ring. But in the end, Romulus had been lucky to escape with his life, had had to turn and flee, alone, for the safety of the Canyon.

But he had his prize now, and that was all that mattered. Luanda. A MacGil. The firstborn MacGil, no less.

Romulus prayed that the legend of the cloak was true, that as soon as he crossed the Canyon with her, the Shield would shatter, and his millions of men waiting outside the Canyon could come rushing in. This time, he would lead them to complete and utter victory against Andronicus, and crush the Ring. Then Romulus would be Supreme Commander, and there would be no one and nothing left to stop him.

Romulus was so close now, he could almost taste it.

As they rode and rode, across the empty, frozen plains, finally, the Eastern Crossing came into view, the high pillars of its entrance marking the horizon. Romulus' horse was near exhaustion, but he kicked even harder, digging his heels in. His destiny was close at hand, and he intended to grab hold of it.

Romulus recalled that, for the cloak to work, he'd have to cross the Canyon with the MacGil on foot. As he reached the base of the Canyon, the entry to the bridge, he stopped abruptly, dismounted, grabbed Luanda, and yanked her down with him.

Somehow, even with her hands bound, Luanda managed to slip out from under him and before he could react, she began to run across the landscape.

In a rage, Romulus reacted quickly, grabbing the whip from his saddle and lashing out at her, wrapping it around her ankles.

Luanda shrieked as he lashed her ankles together, and she fell face first to the ground.

Romulus pulled her roughly towards him, dragging her along the ground. He reached down, grabbed her with one hand, lifted her high into the air, and scowled up at her.

"If you were not a MacGil, I would kill you right now," he seethed.

Luanda grimaced and spat in his face.

Startled, Romulus backhanded her.

Blood sprayed from her lips, and she finally seemed broken; yet Romulus rage was not satisfied. He would tear her apart if he could. Perhaps he would, as soon as they crossed the Canyon. Yes, the thought of that appeased him.

Romulus turned and faced the bridge and draped the cloak over his shoulders. He felt it buzzing, vibrating, felt an energy race through him that he had not felt before. He was certain it was going to work; he would single-handedly take down the Shield. His heart pounded with anticipation.

Romulus reached down and with one arm grabbed Luanda by the waist, hoisting her up and carrying her through the air like an unruly child. He began marching with her onto the bridge.

Luanda bucked and screamed, trying with all her might to get loose. But he held her tight this time, and there was no escape.

Romulus took his first step onto the bridge, and it felt good. Soon he would be across; and despite all the flailing and screaming in the world, there was nothing Luanda could do to stop him.

Soon, the Ring would be his.

CHAPTER THIRTY TWO

Gwendolyn rode beside Argon, Alistair, Aberthol, and Steffen, Krohn at their feet, the five of them on horseback, charging across the northern landscape of the Ring, racing south, for their homeland, for Thor. Gwen was elated to be back in her homeland, back on this side of the Ring, out of the Netherworld. It was like a dream. She had been certain she'd never find Argon, that she'd never escape the Netherworld. And now, here they were, all back home again and so close to being back with Thor.

Gwendolyn kept replaying in her mind the moment Argon had opened his eyes, had come back to her, had come back to life. Tears still poured down her cheeks as she thought of the sacrifice she had made, the dreadful choice she'd had to make to defy fate and bring Argon back. She knew that one day, the time would come to give up what she had promised for Argon's life. Thorgrin's life, or the life of her child.

But that day, at least, was not today.

Gwen's stomach pained her as she rode, the baby turning and turning, as he had been ever since they'd found Argon. It had all been a blur, ever since Argon had been freed. The revived Argon was more powerful than ever, and he used his power to cast a great bubble; Gwen and the others found themselves caught up in it, floating with Argon in the air, skirting over the ground at faster and faster speed, carrying them all the way back through the Netherworld, to the edge of the Canyon—and then floating them harmlessly across it. It had been shocking for Gwendolyn to fly through the air like that. It made her think of her time with Thor, on the back of Mycoples.

Gwen recalled looking down as they crossed the Canyon, marveling at the swirling mists beneath her, the depths of the Canyon which never seemed to end. She wondered if there was even a bottom.

Finally, Argon had set them down back on this side of the Ring, his bubble reaching the end of its power now that they were back safely on this side. They had set down near a group of wild horses they had found roaming the countryside, and they had not stopped riding since.

They raced south and east, heading for the battlefield where Argon had told her he sensed a great battle was taking place. He'd sensed that it was an epic battle for the very heart and soul of the Ring, and that the very future of the Ring was at stake. Surely, she knew, this was where Thor must be. And everyone else she loved and cared for.

Gwen felt a race against time, desperate to get there in time, before it was all too late, before Thor was killed, or anyone else who she loved. She could sense in every ounce of her being that they were all on the edge of a great calamity. Had she been too late in finding Argon? Had it all been for nothing?

There came a screech high above, and she looked up to see Estopheles, circling, leading them.

Gwen kicked her horse harder. Beside her, Krohn snarled, and raced to catch up.

They rode and rode, crossing the Ring, hour after hour passing, all of them knowing what was at stake and none of them even stopping to catch their breath. The sun grew long in the sky, and Gwen's tears never stopped. She felt an awful tragedy was about to happen. Had she sacrificed too much?

They rode deeper and deeper into unknown territory, the Highlands looming large on the horizon. There was a single city striding the peaks, and she recognized it at once from the history books: Highlandia. The McCloud stronghold. The city between two kingdoms.

On the steep mountain slope coming down from Highlandia, Gwen could see the broad trail of an army charging down. And as she followed that trail, and crested a ridge herself, she finally stopped, seeing it. She was shocked.

Stretched out below them, in an immense valley, were thousands of warriors, fighting on both sides. It was the largest battle she had ever seen. On her side, she recognized at once the armor of thousands of Silver and MacGils and Silesian.

But across the valley, she saw they faced a much larger army, a vast number of Empire, tens of thousands of troops pouring in, and an endless stream of reinforcements behind them. Gwen could see even from here the larger-than-life figure of Andronicus, his head rising up in the battlefield, wielding two swords and wreaking havoc as he cut his way through the field. Her people were falling by the hundreds all before her eyes. They were simply outnumbered.

Worst of all, she saw the clearing in the center of the battlefield, the epic one on one battle between two great warriors that all the other warriors seemed to stop and watch. There, alone in the center of the battlefield, fighting one-on-one, was her father's champion, the greatest knight of the Silver: Erec. Normally, she would not fear for him, no matter who he was up against.

But as she looked closely, her heart stopped and her blood ran cold to see his opponent: it was Thorgrin. Her love.

Thor looked like a man transformed, fighting in a blur, faster and stronger than she had ever seen him. He was fighting with all he had, and her heart fell to realize that he aimed to kill Erec.

What had happened to Thor? How could he possibly fight for Andronicus? She could not comprehend it.

Clearly, he was under some sort of magic spell. Gwen felt more confident than ever that finding Argon had been the right thing to do. Clearly, up against this sort of magic, all of them, the entire Ring, would be helpless. It was magic that was needed to fight magic.

Gwen kicked her horse and the others beside her followed. She aimed right for the thick of battle, for the clearing, for Thor. She had to get to Thor in time. She had to save him. She had to save Erec.

"My lady, it is not safe!" Aberthol called out beside her, as they rode. "You charge for battle! Those are real men, with real weapons! You must stop here! You will not reach Thor! You will be killed!"

But Gwendolyn ignored him. She feared not for her own safety. Only for Thor's and for that of the Ring.

"I go where Thor is," she called back. "I fear no man's sword. If you don't want to follow, do not."

"My lady, I am with you!" Steffen said.

"As am I!" Alistair called out.

"I will fight for you, and clear a path for you through those men," Steffen called out. "You will reach Thorgrin!"

Argon rode silently beside her; he did not say anything, but she knew, she saw from the look in his eyes, that he was ready for battle himself.

Gwen's heart pounded and her throat went dry, her baby turning like crazy in her stomach as she neared the impact of battle. Her ears were filled with the clang of metal, of men's death cries, and she could smell the dirt from here. She braced herself as she galloped, not slowing her horse.

Gwen charged into the thick of battle, Steffen leading the way and taking out several men with his arrows. As she rode, MacGils and Silver and Silesians all recognized her, and shouted out with enthusiasm, rallying to rush to her and to part a way for her through the crowd. She was their beloved queen, after all, and now she was a returning hero, with their beloved Argon freed and at her side.

Gwendolyn charged, deeper and deeper into the thick of the battlefield, raising her shield to ward off a blow, her hands shaking. But she never stopped her charge. Empire soldiers pressed in from all sides, realizing an important person had arrived and trying to attack her. One came charging at Gwendolyn with his sword raised high, making it past her entourage, bearing down on her; Gwen waited and then dodged, and he went flying past her.

Another came at her, slipping through the ranks, and this time Steffen charged forward, let loose and arrow, and shot him in the throat. He fell sideways off his horse, dead.

Yet another slipped through, and this one Gwen killed herself, raising her dagger and stabbing him in the throat before he could bring his axe down for her head. He dropped his axe on his own head and collapsed off his horse.

But the crowd grew thicker and thicker as she got closer to Thor, more and more Empire men charging for her. Her men and Steffen did the best they could, killing several of them. But she soon felt herself bumped on all sides, and suddenly, she was slammed on the shoulder by a shield, and knocked off her horse.

Gwen landed hard and rolled. She dropped to her knees, her belly killing her, dirt in her face and in her nose. Gasping, Gwen turned and looked up to see an Empire soldier grimacing, coming down at her with a hammer.

Unable to defend, Gwen raised her hands and braced herself.

The hammer stopped in mid-air, its wielder looking confused.

Gwen looked over and saw Alistair, close by, holding out a single palm, a blue light between her and the weapon. Alistair then raised her hand and directed the light towards the soldier.

The soldier suddenly went flying backwards, dozens of feet through the air, his hammer falling to his side harmlessly.

Alistair reached out a hand and helped Gwen to her feet.

Gwen turned to see several more soldiers charging to attack her, with swords raised high, and she raised a shield and braced her and Alistair from the blows. There came a snarling noise, and Krohn raced past her, leapt into the air, and sunk his fangs into each soldier's throat. Krohn pinned each down and viciously shook his head, until satisfied each was dead.

Krohn, snarling, stood before, scaring back any soldiers who dares approach, and providing an opening for her. Gwendolyn saw her chance. She knew it was now or never.

Gwen sprinted, darting through the thick of men, Thorgrin in sight between the battling men.

She was bumped and banged roughly in each direction, and she dodged more than one below—but her speed worked for her. She was quick, not bogged down by armor, and she managed to weave her way through.

Gwen broke into the open clearing, Krohn leading the way, Steffen and Alistair right behind her, helping to deflect the blows. There, hardly twenty feet away from her, he was.

Thorgrin.

Gwen could hardly breathe, she was so overcome with joy to see him, to be so close to him. She wanted to rush out and give him a hug. She felt like laughing and crying at the same time.

Yet she was also terrified of him. Thor fought with Erec like a man possessed. Watching them fight, two of the greatest warriors of all time, was like watching a work of beauty, the back and forth, the swords clanging, flashing in the light, the speed, the agility, the power, the perfect form. They were two masters of their art, their swords sparkling as if extensions of them, as if they were alive.

Dozens of soldiers stopped fighting and just stood there and watched, mesmerized.

Argon came up beside Gwendolyn, and as he did, he uttered one word:

"Rafi."

Gwendolyn followed his gaze, and saw a sorcerer in scarlet robes standing on the far side of the clearing, watching the spectacle, standing beside Andronicus, beside McCloud. Rafi was the most evil-looking creature that she'd ever seen, and he held out two hands towards Thor, and a scarlet light emanated from them, engulfing him. Suddenly, it all made sense. Thor was under this dark sorcerer's control.

Argon stepped forward, fearlessly, out into the clearing, and held out a palm towards Rafi.

A blue light flew across the clearing, and Rafi turned to see Argon, and his face contorted with fear. Rafi looked shocked and confused.

"Argon," Rafi said darkly. "It cannot be."

The two of them stepped forward, out into the clearing, walking towards each other, each holding out a palm, each directing it at each other as they came closer.

It was a sight to watch, two sorcerers, two titans, facing off with each other, like two mountains colliding. It was a monumental struggle, and Argon's hands shook, as did Rafi's. They were each scowling, gasping for air. They each dropped to their knees, each infusing the other with a different color light.

Finally, Argon let out a great battle cry and raised his hands high, and as he did, Rafi suddenly lifted high into the air. Argon swung both his arms, and Rafi went hurling through the air, flying hundreds of feet, disappearing somewhere into the horizon.

Argon collapsed with the effort.

For a moment, Thor paused in his battle with Erec. He stood there, as if confused, as if a spell had been momentarily broken over him. Thor stared back at Erec with glazed eyes.

Erec, realizing what had happened, paused, too. He stood there, breathing hard, holding out his sword warily.

"Thorgrin, it is I, Erec," he said. "Lay down your arms. It is not too late."

"THORNICUS!" Andronicus yelled, stepping forward. "You are my son! YOU ARE MY SON!" he shrieked.

Thor's eyes glazed over again, and suddenly, he threw himself back into battle, fighting Erec with twice the power, twice the speed.

They exchanged blow after blow, and soon, Erec tripped backwards, landing on one knee, overpowered.

Thor continued to slash for him, slashing with such fury, that he chopped Erec's sword in half. He then knocked Erec's shield from his hand.

Thor stood over Erec, a demonic look in his eyes. He breathed hard, wiped blood from his mouth, and raised his sword to plunge it into Erec.

Gwendolyn could stand to watch no more.

She rushed forward, into the clearing, and ran between Thor and Erec.

"Thorgrin!" she yelled out, tears in her voice. "It's me. Gwendolyn!"

She stood just a foot away from him, crying, tears pouring down her cheeks. She felt overwhelmed with a million emotions.

The entire battlefield stopped to watch.

Thor stood there, sword raised high, and stared back at her. His eyes were not the eyes she knew and recognized and loved. He looked lost to her, lost in another world, another place, another time. As she stood there, for the first time in her life, she felt afraid of him.

"Thorgrin?" she asked, unsure.

Thor grimaced, and pulled his sword back further.

Krohn suddenly rushed forward, snarling, and stood between Thor and Gwen. He snarled back at Thor as if he were a stranger. Gwen could hardly believe it: she had never Krohn snarl at him. Her sense of foreboding increased.

"Thor, it's *me*," she pleaded, tearful. "Gwendolyn. Your love."

Thor blinked, yet still, his eyes held the same blank, confused look.

Gwen prayed that Thor would come back to her, would set down his sword. He seemed as if he might.

But suddenly, he scowled and raised his sword again, and Gwen knew in that moment that she would die by his hands.

Her final thought, before the blow came, was that she would wish for no other way to die in this world.

CHAPTER THIRTY THREE

Mycoples rocked and swayed every which way on the ship as the huge waves crashed all over the deck, sliding her from one side of the deck all the way to the other, slamming into the railing. The sound from the crashing waves was deafening. She tried her best to claw through the net, but the Akron material remained indestructible.

At least the boat was out of control. Huge waves tossed it about, rolling in the seas, the storm that she summoned powerful even beyond her dreams. The boat got sucked in on strong tides and listed its way closer and closer to the Isle of Mist. Mycoples watched it loom closer on the horizon.

The Empire soldiers screamed as they tried to gain control. But they could not. More than one slipped right off the side of the deck, screaming as they plunged to their deaths in the foaming, raging red waters of the sea of blood. More than one monster surfaced, swallowing the men whole.

The boat entered the crashing waves as it neared the shore of the Isle of Mist, a shore comprised of jagged rocks and a narrow strip of sand. The Empire men frantically tried to steer the ship, to avoid the rocks. Somehow, they managed to steer the ship just to the right of them, and they rode one huge, last wave up onto the sandy beach.

It was bad luck for Mycoples. She had wanted them to smash into the rocks, wanted the boat to be destroyed. Now, the boat, while turned on its side and lodged on the beach, was still intact, and half the Empire soldiers along with it.

As they beached, Mycoples, tangled in her net, went flying out the boat, onto the sand. It was a big drop, and the impact hurt, and she struggled frantically to break free.

Yet no matter what she did, the Akron held her in place.

The Empire soldiers, rallying, jumped off the boat, onto shore. They seemed intent not just on saving their lives, but still on torturing her. More than one jumped out with a long spear in hand, and ran for her. They began poking her through the net, hurting her. Even with the howling storm, even being washed up on shore, they still could not stop assaulting her. Her plan had worked only partially: she was still their prisoner. She saw more and more spears coming for her, and she knew that they blamed her. She knew that soon, she would be dead.

There came a sudden roar from high up in the sky, one loud enough to shake the entire island. The Empire men stopped, frozen, and looked to the sky, terrified.

But Mycoples was not terrified. She recognized that sound. She would recognize it anywhere. It was the roar of a dragon. It was one of her own.

Ralibar.

Mycoples heart soared. Ralibar must have smelled the scent of man, and he was coming to see who had arrived.

Mycoples did not know where that left her. Ralibar was a lone and bitter recluse, territorial, and he hated all other dragons. He was rumored to have killed more than one dragon who had dared breach his territory. He might kill these Empire men; but he might kill her, too.

Mycoples was helpless either way. Either way, she seemed destined to die here. At least this way, the Empire men would die, too. At least she would have vengeance. And at least she would die at the hand of another Dragon instead of by a human's hand.

Mycoples heart swelled with anticipation as she heard another roar and looked up and saw Ralibar appear, bursting through the clouds, swooping down in fury. He was large—much larger than she had imagined—and he looked ancient, his red scales faded and cracked with age, and huge, glowing green eyes that she would never forget. His face furrowed into a scowl as he zeroed in on the Empire men.

The Empire soldiers turned and screamed and tried to flee, to run back to their ship.

But it was too late for them. Those who had been fortunate enough to make shore were soon to meet another, much more horrible fate.

Ralibar swooped down, open her great jaws, and breathed fire.

Flames spread through the sky and engulfed the men and ignited the ship. The men shrieked, burned alive. For those he missed, Ralibar swooped down with his huge claws, as thick as a tree trunk, and swiped them in half where they stood. Soon, the beach ran red with blood.

Ralibar's rage was still not satisfied: he dove down, picked up the remnant of the flaming ship with his huge claws, flew at top speed, carrying it through the air, and smashed it into the wall of the cliff.

With a great crash the ship splintered in a million flaming pieces and rained down all around Mycoples.

Mycoples was thrilled. She lay there, stuck inside the Akron net, on the beach, the waves crashing all around her, the last one alive. She looked up at Ralibar, and watched as he turned and set his eyes on her. He paused, hovering there, breathing, black soot coming out of his nostrils, as if debating.

He then let out a screech, and dove down right for her.

Mycoples closed her eyes and braced herself for what was to come. At least she should be happy she saw the Empire men dead, that she had made it this far. At least now, she could die with dignity.

Mycoples heard a whooshing noise, and felt the air rush by as Ralibar dove down for her. She opened her eyes to see him stopped on the beach before her, hovering, flapping his winds. He screeched and arched his back, and she braced herself.

But no blow ever came. She opened her eyes with surprise to see him reach up with his claw and, instead, slice her net.

Mycoples stared back, shocked. Her net was open.

Mycoples leaned back and flapped her wings and arched her back. She was shocked to be free; she had almost forgotten what it felt like. She was even more shocked to realize that Ralibar had freed her, and that he had not killed her, after all.

Ralibar landed on the beach, a few feet away, and stared back at her. She looked into his ancient green eyes, and saw an expression she had never expected to see. It was curiosity. But more than that, there were something else. Like compassion.

Silently, they spoke to each other. Mycoples thanked him, arched her neck and screeched, letting him known her intentions. She was going to fight back, against the Empire. She would fly back immediately, cross the ocean, find a way back into the Ring. She would find a way back through the Shield, find a way to get back to her master, to Thorgrin. He needed her. And that was all that mattered to her.

Ralibar arched back his neck and shrieked, too.

Mycoples took off, into the air, her great wings flapping, and as she did, she heard a great screech behind her. She turned to see Ralibar taking off, catching up to her. She was shocked: he wanted to join her. To help her. Ralibar. The loner. For some reason, he had taken a liking to her.

Mycoples welcomed the company. She flapped her great wings, flying higher and higher, aiming east, for the Ring, for Thorgrin. She sensed he was in mortal danger. And she would do whatever she could to save his life.

CHAPTER THIRTY FOUR

Selese charged with Illepra, the two of them riding with all they had, at the point of exhaustion, not even pausing to rest their horses. They charged down the final stretch of barren landscape and finally, the tall pillars heralding the Eastern Crossing came in sight.

The journey had taken so much out of Selese, more than she could have ever imagined; if it weren't for the thought of losing Reece, she didn't know if she would have been able to press on. She had become stronger and tougher than she had ever imagined, and now that she saw the Eastern Crossing, saw that it was real, she was determined to find Reece, whatever it took. She only prayed that he was here.

As they neared it, Selese was awestruck: the magnificent Eastern Crossing, the one she had heard of ever since she was a child. Of the four crossings bridging the Canyon, the Eastern Crossing was the longest. Being situated on the McCloud side of the Ring, Selese had never been here, and being from a small town, she had never seen anything so big and intimidating in her life. The bridge crossed the Canyon, and it seemed to stretch forever, to another world.

The Canyon itself left her speechless. She had never seen anything in nature remotely like it. A vast chasm in the earth, filled with swirling mists of every color, Selese felt a magical energy coming off of it. She marveled that anything so big and beautiful could exist in the world.

Selese reached the foot of the bridge and she stopped her horse and dismounted, as did Illepra. The two of them stood there, breathing hard, beside their horses.

Selese looked out, and she wondered. She saw no immediate sign of Reece, and her heart sank.

"Perhaps he already crossed?" Illepra asked.

Selese shrugged. She had no idea.

Selese scanned the floor of the bridge, and she saw something which she recognized with her expert eye: blood.

She followed the trail nervously, Illepra beside her. Clearly, a great struggle had taken place here. She only prayed that Reece had not been involved.

As they headed deeper into the bridge, Selese spotted corpses on the ground, and her heart leapt. She prayed none of them were Reece's.

Selese rushed forward, nearly crying as she knelt down, and turned each body over. She breathed deep, so relieved to see that the faces did not belong to Reece. None of these were faces she recognized.

"They bear the markings of the Empire," Illepra observed. "Empire soldiers, all of them," she said, turning them over with her boot. "They were killed by someone."

"By Reece," said Selese, hopeful. "I'm sure he killed them. These men were probably taking the Sword. And he stopped them. As a good knight should."

"And where is he, then?" Illepra asked.

Selese stood there and looked all around, wondering. Could Reece have turned around and gone home, with the Sword? That would be most tragic, if she had ridden all this way for nothing.

Selese went to the railing, laid her palms on it, and stood there and looked out. She sighed, looking down into the mist, and wondered. Was Reece out there somewhere?

As Selese ran her hands along the wide, smooth stone railing of the bridge, she felt something which made her stop and look down. There was, she noticed, a jagged chip in the rail. She noticed blood, and a chunk of the rail knocked off below.

Selese turned and looked at the dead soldiers, and looked back at the markings on the railing, and suddenly, she pieced it all together.

"The boulder," she said. "There was a struggle. It was hoisted over the edge. Look."

Illepra came hurrying over, and Selese leaned over and pointed out the marks the boulder had left.

"Then they must have abandoned the mission," Illepra said. "He must have turned back. Perhaps he's back with the camp even now."

Selese stared down for a long time, and finally, something dawned on her.

"No," she said. "Reece would never abandon a mission. It is not who he is. He did not turn back to safety. He is down there."

Illepra paused, confused.

"Down where?" she asked.

"Down there!" Selese said, pointing. "He descended to the bottom of the Canyon. He went to search for it."

"That is madness!" Illepra said. "Who would do something as crazy as that?"

Selese smiled, proud of him.

"Reece is a man of honor. He would do anything for the sake of the Ring."

She thought, working it out in her mind, and another idea occurred to her.

"He probably went down hastily, as his honor obliged him, but with no plan to ascend. He is trapped. We must go down there. We must help him!"

Illepra shook her head.

"That would be impossible. There is no way down, except for those walls, and I myself cannot climb."

"There's another way," came a voice.

They spun to find an old man standing at the base the bridge, leaning on a cane. He was grizzled, hunched over, with a long white beard and shaggy hair. He wore a ragged cloak and looked as if he'd seen the woes of the world.

"You are brave girls. I cannot deny that. So I will tell you. There's another way down, to save the ones you love."

Selese turned and walked towards him, intrigued, and asked, "What other way?"

"I am the watcher of the Canyon. I see all that goes on here. I saw them descend."

"You did?" Selese asked, wide-eyed.

He nodded.

"They scaled down, without any ropes. You are correct. There is no way out for them. Not without the Linden Rope."

"The Linden Rope?" she asked.

The old man nodded back slowly.

"A way to get down, to the bottom of the Canyon, and to get back up. It has not been used since I was a youth. But I know where it lies; they still keep it in my village. I can lead you to it. The rest is up to you."

Selese surveyed him. He stared back with translucent, knowing eyes. He appeared nearly blind.

"Why would you help us?" Illepra asked, suspicious.

He smiled, revealing only a few teeth.

"I admire courage," he said. "Whether in a man or in a woman. I'm too old for it myself. I'll give you whatever tools you need to express it on your own. Besides, I hate the Empire."

Selese looked to Illepra, as if asking whether to trust him, and she nodded back.

But he was already walking, head low, moving along with his cane, as if expecting them to follow.

CHAPTER THIRTY FIVE

Reece struggled with all his might as he stood there, bound to the post, his wrists and ankles tied behind him, unable to break free. He struggled desperately, and as he looked over he saw all of his legion brothers struggling, too, all equally unsuccessful. They were all lined up, each bound to a tall, wooden pole, ten feet apart from each other, laid out in a semicircle, so that they could see each other. Before them, hardly twenty feet away, they all faced the huge glowing pit of molten lava.

Small and large chunks of lava spewed intermittently out of the hole, and Reece could feel the heat of it even from here, singing his face. As he watched, a small spark of lava went flying in a high arc and landed on his forearm, burning him. He writhed, screaming, as it burned a small hole on his skin.

Sweating, Reece knew they had to do something fast. The Faws had outwitted them, and now they were all their prisoners, facing certain death. Centra was captive, too, but they must have recognized him as a local, because they kept him apart from the others, two Faws holding his arms roughly, his arms bound, while a third jabbed a small dagger at his throat.

As Reece stood there, he scanned their environs, searching for the Destiny Sword. It was still lodged in the boulder, and the boulder, tied to a long rope, was being hoisted, one pull a time, up the far side of the Canyon. Dozens of Faws pulled at it, and with each pull, it climbed higher up the Canyon. It was ascending the wrong side of the Canyon, the eastern side. Reece knew that if it reached the top, the Sword would cross the Canyon. The Shield would be down, and the Ring would be finished.

He had no time. He had to stop them. But Reece had bigger problems: as it was, it appeared that they would not even make it out of here alive.

The Faws spoke to Centra quickly, in a language Reece did not understand, and as they did, they gestured frantically towards Reece.

"They are telling me to give you a message," Centra said. "They want you to know with joy and delight that you are about to be killed. You are to be the sacrifice of the day. They want you to know this before you die, so that you can take satisfaction in knowing that you are food for their god. And they want you to suffer from your death even before you experience it."

Reece half-grinned amidst his pain.

"That's very kind of them," he answered.

"What are they talking about?" O'Connor asked aloud. "What kind of sacrifice?"

Centra spoke back to the Faws in their native language, and they immediately answered him. Centra hesitated, then looked over at the pit with apprehension.

"They plan to throw you into the lava pit—"

Centra paused, clearly not wanting to translate the rest of it, but they, unhappy, jabbed him with the dagger. He continued:

"—and watch as it slowly burns the skin off your bodies."

The group of Faws rose up in a chorus of gleeful laughter, obviously delighted at the spectacle that was about to come. Their laughter was like the chirping of small birds, and it grated on Reece's nerves.

A dozen of these little orange creatures rushed forward and stood facing their leader, who was bigger than all the others and who sat atop a wooden post. The leader said something in a language Reece did not understand, and the others turned and stared at Krog.

"They have decided to kill Krog first," Centra said. "They say the weak must always be sacrificed first."

Krog gulped, writhing to break free.

"Still think it was a good idea to come down here?" Krog called out to Reece.

Reece could not allow this; he knew he had to do something fast.

"Take me first!" Reece screamed out.

The Faws grew quiet as Centra translated.

"Why should they take you?" Centra translated back.

"Tell them that their gods are wrong," Reece called out.

Centra translated, and there came an outraged gasp.

A Faw stepped forward and pointed his dagger in Reece's stomach, hard enough to cause pain. But Reece was undeterred.

"Tell them that great gods require the sacrifice of the strong!" Reece called out, desperate. "Not the weak! You do your god a great dishonor to give him the weak. I am the strongest here. Take me first!"

Centra translated furiously.

There came a long pause, as their leader stared back coldly at Reece. Finally, he nodded at him with a look of respect.

"Perhaps you are right in this," Centra translated. "Yes, you will do just fine."

The Faws let go of Krog and instead turned to Reece.

"Leave him be!" Krog called out.

But the Faws ignored him, and they marched for Reece.

"Pssst!"

Reece heard a hissing noise, and he turned to see Indra, about ten feet away. Her wrists were moving behind her back, ever so slightly, and he looked closely and noticed she held a small dagger hidden in her palm. As she rubbed her wrists up and down, one strand at a time she was severing her twine. They had not bound her ankles, as they had the others, probably because she was a woman.

Indra gave Reece a knowing look, and he gave her one back. *When the time is right*, he whispered to her.

She nodded back knowingly.

The Faws came up behind Reece and hoisted his pole out of the ground with him on it and carried him through the air.

They marched with Reece and the pole over their shoulders, getting closer and closer to the molten pit of lava. As they approached, just feet away, Reece felt the heat growing so strong he had to turn away his face.

Reece was brought closer and closer to the edge of the precipice, and as they raised him high, he felt himself about to be hoisted over the edge.

"It has been nice having you as our guest!" Centra translated.

The chorus of grating laughter, like chirping birds, came again.

Suddenly, there came a scream, and Reece was surprised to realize that it was not his.

Reece saw a dagger lodged in the temple of one of the Faws beside him, who collapsed at Reece's feet.

Reece looked over and saw that Indra had freed herself, and had thrown the dagger expertly and killed the Faw.

Now was his chance. Reece spun around, the pole he was bound to attached to his back, and whacked the other Faws hard in the ribs with the pole, sending them hurtling backwards, screaming, into the glowing lava.

Reece sank to his knees and leaned back against the dagger lodged in the Faw's head. He yanked it out with his fingertips and quickly cut the ropes binding his wrists, then his ankles, freeing himself from the pole.

Several more Faws rushed forward to grab him, but they were surprised as Reece rose up, free, dagger in hand. He stood and charged them, slashing their throats, and stabbing others in the heart.

Indra broke into action. She ran over and freed all the others, cutting their ropes one at a time with her spare dagger. The other Legion wasted no time: they grabbed their weapons, and fought back furiously.

The Faws, though vast in number, were half the size, and not fierce fighters. Their great strength was in numbers, but not in combat. They poured out of the woodwork, from every possible direction, like angry ants, and leapt on their backs with their claws and sharp teeth, causing scratches and bites.

But Reece and his men were undeterred, brave warriors who had faced worse, and they each managed to fight and push them all back.

Dozens of Faws fell all around them.

Yet still the Faws kept coming, thousands of them, pouring in from all sides of the cliffs, from caves. There came a never-ending stream, and Reece realized this would not be easy. Despite their strength, they were vastly outnumbered. He had to act fast. He had to retrieve the Sword and get them all out of there as soon as he could.

Reece turned, scanning for the Sword, and saw that the boulder was well up the side of the Canyon, and still being hoisted. He had to stop it. He could not let it reach the top.

"Cover me!" Reece yelled.

Elden, O'Connor, Indra, Serna and Conven rushed forward, circling around him, clearing a path for him with their swords as Reece charged for the canyon wall. Reece let out a great battle cry and slashed furiously with his sword, as he cut his way through dozens of Faws, the crowd getting thicker by the moment.

Reece finally reached the Canyon wall, and as he did, he leapt up onto a foothold in the slippery rock, and climbed his way high enough up the Canyon to be out of reach of the Faws. The boulder with the Sword in it was perhaps twenty feet above him, and Reece realized he needed to sever the rope. He drew his sword, leaned back, and prepared to chop it down.

Suddenly, a Faw scaled the wall, grabbed his ankle, and yanked Reece backwards. Reece slipped, and he went falling through the air and landed on the ground, on his back, winded.

Reece glanced over and saw the boulder was now too far out of reach, the ropes too high for him to cut. And now the wall was swarming with Faws. He'd lost his chance.

He had an idea.

"O'Connor, your bow!" Reece shouted, as he fended off his attackers.

O'Connor kicked two Faws out of his way, and followed Reece's glance and saw what he was getting at. O'Connor reached back for his bow and took aim. He fired off a shot, aiming for the rope, as Reece had intended.

It missed by a foot. O'Connor was attacked by more Faws, knocking him to the ground, and Reece and Elden rushed forward and killed them.

"Help!" Krog called out.

Reece turned to see Krog doing his best to fight them off, but limping heavily on one leg. Two Faws were on his back, trying to bite his neck.

Reece rushed forward, as did Indra, and at the same time they each knocked a Faw off, Reece using the edge of his hilt, and Indra stabbing one in the back.

Krog looked at Reece with gratitude.

Reece rushed back to O'Connor's side, helping fight off the Faws and helping him regain his feet.

O'Connor grabbed his bow, took aim once again, hands shaking, and fired three more shots with his last three arrows.

On the third and final shot, there came the sound of snapping twine, as he landed a perfect, impossible shot.

There came a great whooshing noise, and suddenly the boulder came hurling down, like a meteor from the sky, and crashed into the Canyon floor with a huge reverberating thud.

Reece was elated. They had stopped it from rising to the wrong side of the Canyon wall. Now they had to get it and get out.

"The Sword, quick!" Reece called out.

He and his men fought their way towards it, through the Faws, attacking left and right, until they finally all made their way to the boulder. Elden and O'Connor held the front line, fighting Faws off, while Reece and the others reached down and tried to hoist the boulder.

But it was too heavy. It wouldn't budge.

All around them, more and more Faws were closing in.

"Those poles!" O'Connor said. "I saw them hoist it earlier. The weight of the Sword is heavy—but only if touched directly. If we use a barrier, like poles, it lightens its weight."

Reece joined with Conven and Indra and Serna and Krog as they jammed the poles beneath the boulder. As one, they all began to move it.

Reece was shocked; O'Connor was right. The Sword was not meant to be touched by the human hand. But with an intermediary, like wooden poles, they could hoist the boulder like any other rock.

They hoisted the boulder onto their shoulders with the poles, and began to march away with it.

Reece saw they were in trouble. They had, despite all odds, achieved the impossible; but now, there was no possible way out. There were thousands of Faws before them, more and more pouring in, and it was a long hike to the other side of the Canyon, and an even harder hike to get up. *If* they could even get the Sword up. They couldn't do it under combat. In fact, they'd be lucky to even fight their way out of here alive.

There was just no way to bring the Sword. And yet, at the same time, Reece knew they could not just leave it here, could not return empty-handed. And they could not leave it in the hands of the Faws, who would let it rise in the other side of the Canyon, and lower the Shield.

Reece frantically surveyed his surroundings, desperate for a solution.

And then, suddenly, he had one.

Reece saw the glowing lava pit, in the center of the battlefield, and as much as it pained him, he knew he had no choice. If he could not bring the Sword back, he would have to destroy it.

But would destroying the Sword for all time destroy the Ring, too? Would it destroy the Shield? He did not know. But he had no other choice. It was a desperate situation, and all he knew was that if he did nothing, then the Sword would definitely get in the wrong hands, and the Shield would definitely lower, and the Ring would definitely be destroyed.

He had to risk the uncertainty.

"TO THE LAVA!" Reece commanded.

With one last desperate push, Reece and the others bore the boulder on their shoulders and marched their way towards the pit, Elden and O'Connor fighting off the Faws all around them. Every step was a struggle on the muddy Canyon floor. Foot by foot they slogged their way through, and soon, Reece's face was hot with the glow of the lava.

They stood there, at the precipice, arms shaking, and Reece looked down at the molten fire.

The others realized, with horror, what he was about to do.

"Are you sure you want to do this?" O'Connor screamed.

Reece was not sure. But there was no other way out.

"INTO THE LAVA!" Reece commanded.

They all followed orders, and as one, they all began to hurl it over. Reece felt the tremendous weight on his shoulders and arms as they hoisted the boulder and hurled it, the Sword in it, over the edge, into the molten pit of fire.

As it sank, the entire earth quaked beneath them, the greatest earthquake Reece had ever felt, strong enough to knock them all off of their feet.

And as Reece watched it melt, he stared into the flames, and all he could think was: *what have I done?*

CHAPTER THIRTY SIX

Thor stood there, sword in hand, facing Gwendolyn, who knelt before him, eyes swollen with tears. He tried to remember. He saw her face, and in some dim part of himself, it meant something to him. But he could not remember what. Did he know her?

All about them, in the broad clearing, soldiers on both sides stopped their fighting, all staring, the war at a standstill as Thor faced Gwen, the Queen of the MacGils. Thor looked into her eyes, beautiful eyes, examined her face, and he tried to summon it.

Something came back to him……flashes…he was not sure what. He could not piece it together.

"Thorgrin, it's me," Gwen said, crying. "Come back to me. It's Gwendolyn. I love you. I'm so sorry for everything I said. You are nothing like your father. I love you. I *love* you."

Thor stood there, sweat rolling into his eyes, and his hands shook as he held the sword over her. A part of him understood her; but another part of him had no recognition.

"THORNICUS, MY SON!" Andronicus boomed. "Do not believe her! She is the enemy. The enemy of your father. She is filled with lies. She has come to betray you. If you are my one and only son, you must answer me now. Kill this woman. Kill her for me. Kill her, and prove your loyalty to me once and for all time."

Thor heard his father's words, and they resonated through him, like a command that controlled his limbs, that he could not shake. It was as if he had spoken the words himself. They were more than a command. They were like his own will, spoken aloud.

Stood there, arms shaking, and finally, he knew what he had to do. His father had spoken. And that was all that mattered now.

Suddenly, Krohn snarled and leapt for Thor.

Thor spun and reacted with his battle skills; he backhanded Krohn with his gauntlet. Krohn yelped and went flying sideways through the air. Gwendolyn cried out as Krohn landed on his side, several feet away, whining.

Thor raised his sword again, this time to strike the final blow. For his father. It was time to be his one and only true son forever.

Whatever it took. Gwen wept, but it no longer mattered. Thor had to do what he had to do.

"THORGRIN!"

A voice cut through the air, forcing Thor to stop. It was a female voice, one he did not recognize. One he had never heard, yet which seemed so deeply familiar.

Thor turned and saw a woman emerge from the crowd. She approached him slowly, her wide blue eyes locked on his, as she walked all the way through the clearing without flinching, staring at him.

She stood beside Gwendolyn. She lay a soft palm on Gwendolyn's shoulder, and continued staring at Thor with intensity, her eyes shining right through him.

"You cannot harm her," the woman said, calm, confident, authoritative. "You cannot harm her because I command you. I, Alistair, command you."

Thor looked into her eyes, and the sound of her voice resonated through Thor's body, fighting inside him, counteracting Andronicus's voice. It was the most intense sound he'd ever heard in his life, and the vibration did something to him he could not understand. Somehow, it was breaking the hold on him, breaking his father's spell. For the first time, he was beginning to gain clarity. He felt as if a fog was lifting, as if many layers were slowly being peeled back.

Thor wanted her to speak more—he *craved* for her to speak more.

"Alistair," he repeated.

Somehow, the name rang through his head. He did not know why.

"Thorgrin," Alistair said, "you will not harm her, because that is not who you are. That is who Andronicus wants you to be. But you are not your father. You are Thorgrin, of the Western Kingdom. You are not your father and you are not your mother. You are your own man. I know this, because I know you."

Thor blinked, sweat stinging his eyes, as a battle raged within him. The more she spoke, the more he felt Andronicus' influence waning. Thor stood there, wavering with the sword, his hands shaking violently.

"Thorgrin," she said, stepping forward, laying a gentle palm on his wrist. As she did, Thor could not resist. Slowly, he felt himself lowering his sword, relaxing in her grasp.

Somehow, she was the only one. The only one who could get through to him. She held some energy, something he could not understand. With every word she spoke, it made him come back more to himself, to see the real situation before him.

Thor looked around, and for the first time, he was overwhelmed with clarity. He saw Gwendolyn, the one and only true love of his life, kneeling before him, crying. He saw himself, with utter horror, holding a sword, pointing it at her. He saw Krohn, whining, lying on his side. He saw himself facing off against his own people.

It was more than he could take. Thor despised himself. He wanted to run the sword through his own heart; he would rather kill himself than ever point it at Gwendolyn. He felt a tear run down his cheek, felt an awful guilt begin to well up inside of him. He felt as if he'd betrayed them all, all of his people, all the ones who loved him most.

Most of all, Gwendolyn. The woman he'd loved more than he could possibly say. He wanted to drop to his knees and beg her forgiveness, to beg everyone's forgiveness.

Thor turned and looked at Alistair, and as his eyes locked with hers, he felt himself awash with new layers of clarity. Finally, the veil was lifted. Finally, Thor was returning to himself. Who was this woman?

"Thorgrin, you will not harm anyone," she said, "because you are not of them. You are one of us. I know this, because I know you. I know this, because you and I, we share the same father. And the same mother."

She looked deep into his eyes, and he felt entranced. He felt he was on the verge of a great revelation, one that would change his entire life forever. As he stared, the earth, the entire Ring, suddenly quaked, the ground shaking violently, inexplicably, as if some cosmic event had just taken place, as if the Ring were about to split in two.

But not before Alistair could say one last thing:

"I know this, Thorgrin, because I am your sister."

A SKY OF SPELLS
Book #9 in the Sorcerer's Ring

"A breathtaking new epic fantasy series. Morgan Rice does it again! This magical sorcery saga reminds me of the best of J.K. Rowling, George R.R. Martin, Rick Riordan, Christopher Paolini and J.R.R. Tolkien. I couldn't put it down!"
--Allegra Skye, Bestselling author of SAVED

In A SKY OF SPELLS (BOOK #9 IN THE SORCERER'S RING), Thorgrin finally returns to himself and must confront his father once and for all. An epic battle occurs, as two titans face each other, and as Rafi uses his power to summon an army of undead. With the Destiny Sword destroyed, and the fate of the Ring in the balance, Argon and Alistair will need to summon their magical powers to help Gwendolyn's brave warriors. Yet even with their help, all could be lost if it were not for the return of Mycoples, and her new companion, Ralibar.

Luanda struggles to prevail against her captor, Romulus, as the fate of the Shield hangs in the balance. Reece, meanwhile, struggles to lead his men back up the Canyon walls, with Selese's help. Their love deepens; but with the arrival of Reece's old love, his cousin, a tragic love triangle and misunderstandings develop.

When the Empire is finally ousted from the Ring, and Gwendolyn has her chance for personal vengeance against McCloud, there is great cause to celebrate. As the new Queen of the Ring, Gwen uses her powers to unite both MacGils and McClouds for the first time in history, and to begin the epic rebuilding of the land, of her army, and of the Legion. King's Court slowly comes back to life once again, as they all begin to pick up the pieces. It is destined to become a more glorious city than even her father ever dreamed of, and in the process, justice finally finds Gareth.

Tirus must be brought to justice, too, and Gwen will have to decide what sort of leader she will be. There is a great conflict amongst Tirus' sons, not all of whom see things the same way, and a struggle for power erupts once again, as Gwen decides if she will accept an invitation to the Upper Isles, thus making the MacGil clan whole once again. Erec is summoned to return to his people in the Southern Isles and see his dying father, and Alistair joins him, as they prepare for their wedding. Thorgrin and Gwendolyn may have wedding preparations in their future, too.

Thor becomes closer to his sister, and as all settles down inside the Ring, he finds himself summoned to embark on his greatest quest of all: to seek out his mysterious mother in a faraway land and to find out who he really is. With multiple wedding preparations in the air, with Spring returning, King's Court rebuilding, festivals afoot, peace seems to settle back onto the Ring. But danger lurks in the most unforeseen corners, and all of these characters greatest tribulations might be yet to come.

With its sophisticated world-building and characterization, A SKY OF SPELLS is an epic tale of friends and lovers, of rivals and suitors, of knights and dragons, of intrigues and political machinations, of coming of age, of broken hearts, of deception, ambition and betrayal. It is a tale of honor and courage, of fate and destiny, of sorcery. It is a fantasy that brings us into a world we will never forget, and which will appeal to all ages and genders.

"Grabbed my attention from the beginning and did not let go….This story is an amazing adventure that is fast paced and action packed from the very beginning. There is not a dull moment to be found."
--Paranormal Romance Guild {regarding Turned}

"Jam packed with action, romance, adventure, and suspense. Get your hands on this one and fall in love all over again."
--vampirebooksite.com (regarding Turned)

About Morgan Rice

Morgan is author of the #1 Bestselling THE SORCERER'S RING, a new epic fantasy series, currently comprising eleven books and counting, which has been translated into five languages. The newest title, A REIGN OF STEEL (#11) is now available!

Morgan Rice is also author of the #1 Bestselling series THE VAMPIRE JOURNALS, comprising ten books (and counting), which has been translated into six languages. Book #1 in the series, TURNED, is now available as a FREE download!

Morgan is also author of the #1 Bestselling ARENA ONE and ARENA TWO, the first two books in THE SURVIVAL TRILOGY, a post-apocalyptic action thriller set in the future.

Among Morgan's many influences are Suzanne Collins, Anne Rice and Stephenie Meyer, along with classics like Shakespeare and the Bible. Morgan lives in New York City.

Please visit www.morganricebooks.com to get exclusive news, get a free book, contact Morgan, and find links to stay in touch with Morgan via Facebook, Twitter, Goodreads, the blog, and a whole bunch of other places. Morgan loves to hear from you, so don't be shy and check back often!

Books by Morgan Rice

THE SORCERER'S RING
A QUEST OF HEROES (BOOK #1)
A MARCH OF KINGS (BOOK #2)
A FEAST OF DRAGONS (BOOK #3)
A CLASH OF HONOR (BOOK #4)
A VOW OF GLORY (BOOK #5)
A CHARGE OF VALOR (BOOK #6)
A RITE OF SWORDS (BOOK #7)
A GRANT OF ARMS (BOOK #8)
A SKY OF SPELLS (BOOK #9)
A SEA OF SHIELDS (BOOK #10)
A REIGN OF STEEL (BOOK #11)

THE SURVIVAL TRILOGY
ARENA ONE (Book #1)
ARENA TWO (Book #2)

the Vampire Journals
turned (book #1)
loved (book #2)
betrayed (book #3)
destined (book #4)
desired (book #5)
betrothed (book #6)
vowed (book #7)
found (book #8)
resurrected (book #9)
craved (book #10)

CPSIA information can be obtained at www.ICGtesting.com
Printed in the USA
LVOW10s1558080915

453276LV00001B/29/P